Bob Moats

I0568110

Made for TV Murders

Made for TV Murders

ISBN – 978-0-9903138-0-9

For information and address:
Magic 1 Productions
P.O. Box 524, Fraser MI 48026-0524
Website: http://murdernovels.com
Cover by Bob Moats

Bob Moats

Other Jim Richards series books by Bob Moats

For a preview or to purchase a book, go to
http://murdernovels.com

What a few people are saying about Murder Novels by Bob Moats

Mr. Moats, I just got your novel "Classmate Murders" and have to let you know, I read it in one evening. That is the first book I have ever done that with. That was the most enjoyable book I have ever read. I just started reading e-books, and reading again, after getting my wife a Kindle. This book was my 12th, and the best. I just got Las Vegas Showgirls to (read) tomorrow evening. I look forward to reading many of your books in this series. I have been searching for an author and books that were fun, entertaining reads. Your books are just the ticket.

Regards, A new fan, Bill from South Carolina

****

Another very nice comment submitted through my website from Micki P.:

"I recently was given a kindle for my 60th birthday. The first book I downloaded was the Classmate Murders and have now read every one of the them. Today I started on the Fatal Rejection series. Thank you for the wonderful ride with Jim and Penny and all the rest of the troop. I have laughed and giggled thru the stories, my poor family gave me the strangest looks! Now I really want a little Yorkie!! Fatal Rejection so far is another great read! I will be looking out for more of Jim Richards and since you are my #1 Author, anything of yours I can find."

Author's Note:

Please read "Classmate Murders" before reading this book. This story is about the fictional filming of a movie that is based on a book written by Jim Richards about the classmate murders. There are many spoilers in this book that give the plot away to my first book, so please read that before this book.

Thanks, Bob Moats

Made-For-TV Murders
By Bob Moats

Chapter 1

I was sitting quietly in my office one morning when Hollywood walked in.

Okay, to explain, we need to go back just over a year, when I first became involved in the classmate murders, or more correctly, cheerleader murders. I became involved in the hunt for two serial killers who were stalking and killing the cheerleaders from my old high school, although forty years later. The first cheerleader murdered was an old childhood flame that I knew when I was in eighth grade, I hadn't seen her in over forty years and she turned up strangled in her shower, while the police were watching her. Well, not actually watching her in the shower, but while she was in protective custody. Then four more aging, former cheerleaders were murdered while in protective custody, which drove homicide detective Will Trapper just about nuts. He was the primary investigator on the case back then, and I became a bug in his attempts to find the killers. We did finally track down and took out the killers, and Penny was the last of the cheerleaders and the only one to survive. Happily for me.

After the basic story was released to the national media, I had decided to sit at my laptop and write the whole detailed account into a novel, so I spent a year, on and off, putting it all down into book form that I finally finished about two months ago. I had found a few contacts in the industry and managed to find a book agent to finally get around to reading the thing. Funny thing is the media, news, television, blogs and such had spread the story about the crazed killers and their leader, who all ended up dead, leaving a female Detroit TV talk show hostess as the last unharmed victim, so my book was very relevant. It was finally published.

Before I even started writing the book, the story released by the media was big, and back then we had been approached by a few TV network producers who wanted to put the whole incident into a mini-series movie for television, but nothing ever came of it. Mostly because the producers needed everyone involved to allow their part in the story to be told. There were a few hold-overs on giving permission to have them portrayed, but then when my book came out, it was now a way to film the story based on the book. It's amazing what you can write about people as long as you don't mention real names without permission. But back then the movie wasn't a go project. Until today.

So when my office door flew open on that morning and in walked three men in suits, I thought the FBI was invading my space. The lead man held out a card, which I took carefully and gazed at the name and company, James Drury, Really Big Show Pictures, Los Angeles, California.

"I presume you are Mr. Richards, Jim Richards?" He spoke as his two followers stood quietly by.

"I am, and what can I do for you?" I replied, hoping from seeing the Really Big Show Pictures printed on the card, they were here to talk book options for a film.

"As you see from my card, I'm with a film production company and we want to talk to you about your book, Classmate Murders." He answered my thoughts.

I was already spending my film residuals on a villa in the Barbados, "I'm listening." I said simply, so not to queer the deal. "Please have a seat." I motioned to the client chairs, the lead man, Drury, sat at the front chair, his henchmen sat back by the wall on my extra chairs. They had a grim look to them, must be the Michigan weather after just coming from the sunny west coast.

"Mr. Richards, you not only wrote the book about the two serial killers, but you also lived it. I'm impressed. My company directors have sent me to see if we can come to some agreement, so we can put your ordeal on film, which will be presented on the TNT Network. It will be a made for television mini-series. Have you been approached by any other production companies?" he said with a smile on his face, looking like a vulture waiting for the soon to be carcass to take its last gasp.

"About a year ago, yes, before I wrote my book, but I haven't had the pleasure to be approached by the industry recently, you are the first." I smiled back, trying to keep from becoming a carcass.

"Have you considered the film usage of your book?" He never broke the smile, his lips barely moving while he talked, reminding me of a ventriloquist.

"It has crossed my mind." Several times in fact.

"We are authorized to talk a deal with you for the rights to put your book to film, and I hope we can come to some arrangement." he spoke like a lawyer. I wasn't fond of lawyers, I'd rather he talk like a guy sitting in a bar talking to me about the weather.

"Mr. Drury, cut to the chase, what is the deal, and how much control will I have over the script writing?" I had heard horror stories about authors' books being taken to film and butchered. I was stunned to watch the TV movie of a Robert Parker book about Police Chief Jesse Stone, the movie had very little in comparison with the book other than the title and character names. "As you know Classmate Murders is a true story, it's not good to fool with the truth, or embellish it to make it exciting. The whole thing as I lived it was exciting, and scary, as it played out. It would make a great film as is. Just how much of a say would I have in the production of the thing?"

"Well, we are open for your input, after all you were there. We could bring you on as technical advisor as well as the story author. I'm sure you would need to be on hand while our writers would put the story into a screenplay, to keep the authenticity of it intact. I'm sure we could even give you a producing credit."

They were throwing me a bone to get me to give in. "As technical advisor, how much weight would my voice have in the scheme of things. I would make a suggestion and the director would say that's nice, but we'll do it his way. I don't want the thing to turn into some director's vision of the story, he or she wasn't there."

Drury was quiet for a bit, "You are quite right Mr. Richards. I'm impressed as to your integrity of the incident."

"It was very personal to me, I had friends die terrible deaths and I was almost killed to boot. I want the film to show that terror that was felt by all concerned." I said.

Drury was silent again, then took a breath and spoke, "I do hope we can come to some agreement, I really enjoyed your book, I did read it as I do any book we consider for filming. I can see you would bring an honest eye to it and I'm ready to talk options."

I stood and went to my office door, I hung out the sign saying I was not available; I had a number of signs for my actions, and locked the door. I came back to my chair and said. "Let's talk."

Bob Moats

For the next two hours we haggled about what they wanted and what I wanted for the production of my book. I had a producing credit that I insisted was more than just honorary; I had to have a say in the thing. He agreed, but with conditions, that the other producers had to be in on the process. I thought that was like saying I was the only Democrat in a room full of Republicans, who wins? We talked about how the book would be transformed into script and I wanted my say about what the actors would say and how the plot went along, Drury agreed reluctantly.

All during this grueling process, his two assistants were busy writing down our agreements and conditions, and then we finally came to an agreeable point, where we were both happy with everything. Drury said they would have a contract written up and a check for the rights to their options to the book. I was holding my breath when I thought about the agreed on two hundred grand that they offered. I would have held out for half, I wasn't greedy, but two hundred thousand dollars sounded so much better. I even managed to finagle a percentage of the profits later on when the film was released. Being as it was a made for television movie, the profits wouldn't be as great as a theatrical release, but I did manage to get a percentage of the DVD video sales and rentals. I was very happy.

The three men took their leave and departed. I just now had to break the news to Penny, and I could almost see her packing her bags for a round the world vacation.

*

Chapter 2

On my way home, I called Penny and told her not to surprise me with anything from her show today; she said unfortunately she had nothing to hit me with, which was good. I said I had some people coming over, since I called our friends from the office to stop by the house tonight. I had something important to tell everyone, and it also involved Deacon out in Vegas. I would put him on our speaker phone when I was ready to make my announcement. She asked me what it was and I told her to be patient and she would know the same time everyone else did.

"I hope you're announcing your retirement from fighting crime," she laughed.

"Not as long as there is crime in the world, what would they do without me."

"Okay, I had hoped that would be it, but you say it's something everyone will want to hear?"

I could see her wheels turning in her head and I said, "Don't try to figure it out, just go with it and you'll know soon enough. I have to stop by the store and get some refreshments for our guests. I'll see you soon."

I hung up before she could badger me further and went to the nearest party store and did my shopping. I packed the goodies into the car and went home. I had to park next to the Lincoln Town Car that the mob had sent me. Well, actually it came from Francis and don Gino Traviano as a gift for saving the life of their new niece, Marina, while I was out in New York City fighting crime. I bought a car cover for the huge car; it was just short of being a full stretch limo, one that could be driven by me, alone, or with a chauffeur. I loved it. I put the extra car cover over my newly restored twenty year old Crown Vic and tied it down. I stood looking at the garage where we put Penny's car, and thought about putting an addition on to it so all the cars would be out of the lousy Michigan weather. Then again, maybe we could just buy a new house, better yet, a mansion out in Vegas and get away from Michigan weather all together. Something to think about now that I was becoming a big time author and owner of a mini-limo.

I had taken all the refreshments out of the car before covering it and took them into the house. Penny met me at the door and was bouncing around me asking what I was going to announce. I asked if she could take some of the packages from my arms and she did, then after putting them on the snack bar, she turned to me and gave me a good tonsil search with her tongue, after which I said I still wasn't talking. She pouted and sat on a stool at the snack bar and just stared at me. I was feeling the daggers she was throwing with her eyes and said to stop that. She bent down and picked up Willy for me to kiss; I said I don't kiss doggie lips and patted

Made for TV Murders

Willy on the head. He squirmed in Penny's arms, so I took him from her and he settled down.

"I guess we know who he likes." Penny said.

"Us males have to stick together."

"Can't you give me a hint?" she said after a moment of silence.

I enjoyed watching her squirming, "Okay, it has to do something with my book."

"Oh my gosh, did you make the New York Times best seller list?"

"I only wish. No, not yet, but someday soon I hope. It will look good on my book covers." Changing the subject, "Oh, and I started writing about the showgirl case out in Vegas, started it today at the office. I can write better there than here, you're too distracting." I smirked.

"I beg your pardon, I'm not distracting." she said forcefully.

"I can't concentrate with your great body walking around the house; I want to jump you every time I see you."

"Better remember that stud. I don't put out for just anyone." she smiled and cupped her hands under her breasts and bounced them for me.

"Quit that, we have company coming soon."

Just as I said that there was a knock at the door, it was Buck. He made his trademark walrus smile and I invited him in.

Penny gave him a hug and said, "Jim is being mean, he won't tell me what his secret is."

"I could beat it out of him." Buck said to Penny.

"No, I need him alive for later tonight." she laughed.

"I'm right here people. Buck have a seat, I got you diet Sprite, want one now?" He said he did and I went to the fridge and took one out for him. It was only 6:00 but I decided that my news was a reason to celebrate so took out a can of beer. I yelled to Penny asking if she wanted one, she did. I came back out to the family room and handed out the refreshments.

"This must be something really special for you to start drinking beer before 8:00. Buck, go ahead and beat it out of him."

"Just wait for Trapper and Becker to get here. Then you can all beat on me."

On cue the doorbell rang and it was Trapper with Barry Becker. I greeted them and told them to come in. I said there was beer and pop in the fridge and to help themselves, they did.

Made for TV Murders

Everyone was seated comfortably in the room and I dialed the phone for Deacon. It was only 3 P.M. in Vegas, so I hoped I didn't get him at the police station. He came on and I said, "How's crime in Sin City?"

"Jimmy! How the hell are you?" he said and then I heard him say it was me, probably to Lynn. I then heard her yell out to me. "What are you calling for so early in the day?" she asked.

"Remember, it's three hours later here, and I got Penny, Buck, Trapper and Becker here with me."

"Wow, what's the occasion and hi to everyone." he said and then he put me on the speaker phone in Lynn's office. Lynn warned me that she could hear, so be careful what I say.

"I invited everyone to our home, and called you guys, to announce that my Classmate Murders book is being made into a movie, just made the deal today."

Everyone went nuts, yelling and congratulating me. Penny bounced over and plopped down on my lap and kissed me hard.

Trapper asked, "Who's fronting the film?"

"Some LA company called Really Big Show Pictures. They are one of the companies involved, it's for a made for TV movie for the TNT Network.

"I've never heard of them, I'll run a check to be sure they are legit." Trapper offered.

"Yeah, I guess that would be a good idea, to be sure I'm not being scammed. Thanks."

Deacon came back over the phone, "Hey, if they are out here on the west coast, I can check that right now, be back shortly, talk to Lynn."

Lynn asked, "Have they said anything about casting?"

"No, just getting the commitments for book rights ironed out first, then they'll be coming back with a contract to sign and a check to make Penny rich when I keel over."

Penny whacked me and said to stop that. "I don't even want your money, it's not funny."

"Sorry, I'm just a bit overwhelmed by their offer for the book, two hundred thousand dollars." Everyone made noises when they heard that.

"Okay, I take it back; put that in your will." Penny grinned.

Buck finally spoke, "I want to see Hulk Hogan play me. He said he might do it when I met him out in Vegas during Penny's convention."

"I don't know who will be playing any parts, but since it's a made for TV movie, the cast will probably be lesser known actors or one's that haven't been acting in a while. They can be hired for lower pay. No big budget film here. Maybe they'll let all of us play ourselves, that would be interesting."

Deacon announced he was back and said "I called a cop friend out in LA and he has heard of their operation, it's legit, they do a lot of made for television movies, low budget ones but they do get air time on the cable networks. Couple of their films made it big in the Emmy nominations for mini-series."

I was impressed. So was everyone else.

"I appreciate everyone here giving me permission to use your real names in my book; I hope you will let the movie people have that same privilege?" I said.

Trapper spoke up, "I don't mind at all having my name associated with this production, it kind of makes me a household name that way and maybe even get me in a few doors, when I say who I am." He grinned as everyone agreed.

I knew he was right; a couple of times during my cases, the mention of the Classmate or Bridezilla murders earned me a little respect from law officers. I had no problem with it and with this movie we were going to be well known now.

*

Chapter 3

We partied into the night, I decided not to go into work tomorrow, I had no cases and Drury told me as he was leaving, they'd be back in a few days. I gave him my card and said to call me when they were ready.

Penny was on my lap most the night, I think she had a few more beers than I did, she was getting a bit frisky. I finally had to chase everyone out so Penny and I could do our own celebrating before she passed out. Lucky for me she didn't.

Early the next morning, Penny was skittering around the house getting ready for work. She only bumped into the walls a few times; I had to laugh watching her trying to pretend she wasn't hung over. I told her to be real careful driving to work, then I asked if she wanted me to drive her and she got indignant and said she was capable of driving herself. I told her she could leave Willy home today as I wasn't going into the office.

"Oh, now that you're a famous author with money, you feel you can just lie around the house?" She whined.

"I'm just taking a break; I'll go back in tomorrow. I just want to spend some quality time with Willy; we haven't had much father and son bonding in a while. And it will give you a chance to not worry about him at work."

Made for TV Murders

"I don't worry about him; the make-up girls take good care of him and pamper him when I do my show." She retorted.

"Right there, he gets too much face time with females, he needs a man to balance out his psyche. I don't want our little guy to start wearing make-up and dresses." I smiled.

She just stared at me, then put on her coat and said, "Fine, now I'll have to return that cute little skirt and blouse I got for him. You can take him shopping and get him some pants and a leather jacket. Then you can take him to visit Luther and his motorcycle buddies and turn Willy into a tough biker." She picked up her bag and purse and kissed me, then headed towards the door.

She stopped before she went out, "I'm going to get a female dog, so I can pamper her. Then you two can go run the streets and act macho. Later." Then she went out.

I sat laughing for a bit then looked at Willy, "You want to go look at motorcycles?" Willy bounced around my lap as we sat on the couch. I got up holding on to him and went to get his leash, then we went out in the back yard for a walk. We stopped letting him run loose out there ever since he ran off into the woods next to our property and we had a hell of a time trying to find him in the tall brush. Willy wasn't the most obedient dog and had a mind of his own, so to call him for anything other than food was a waste of time. I wondered if dog training would help, I would look into that.

We went down by the dock and stood just looking out at the water of Lake St. Clair. It was unusually calm today; just a sheet of glass but occasionally a motor boat would fly by breaking up the still waters. I sat on the dock and Willy nestled next to me, it was a bit cold out this morning, mostly dampness, which I hated. I longed for the dry heat of Vegas, maybe someday.

My cell phone rang and it was Trapper. "Hey, chief, what's up?"

"I just got a call from our friend, Earl Daws. He said since you guys got back from your New York adventure, he has been mulling over becoming a private investigator himself. You don't mind some competition do you?"

"No, there's enough cheating spouses out there to go around, maybe he and I can hook up and start our own agency. You could join us too, after you retire." I grinned at the thought of the three of us perverts on surveillance watching a husband fooling around with a mistress.

"Yeah, it's a thought. Anyway, I just wanted to know if you heard anything yet on the movie?"

"It's 8:00 in the morning, LA is still around 5:00 in the morning. I doubt that they are even out of bed yet. Be patient and I'll call you when I hear something."

Made for TV Murders

"Okay, I'm just a little anxious to finally see this thing get produced. They teased us enough a year ago with their plans to film it and nothing ever came of it. Keep me informed, later." He said and hung up. I noticed he still didn't say good-bye, but now he was saying 'later' as he hung up. At least I knew when he was finished talking now.

I looked at Willy as he just stared out at the water and I hoped we weren't going to have to wait long for this to all come together. I stood, then Willy jumped up and we went back to the house. We came in through the porch and I stopped to stare at the stripper pole Penny had installed from her show. I grabbed it and tried to do a spin around it, but fell down almost crushing Willy, who luckily ran off before I came to a thud on the floor. I decided that I wasn't a very good stripper so I just ambled around the house; it was a bit strange to be alone in the house without Penny around. I realized that I was never here while she was away, and it was now a bit too quiet,

Penny always made her presence felt, even when she was asleep. I was starting to miss her and she had only been gone for over an hour. I wondered why I didn't miss her this much while I was out at my office; I guess my work kept my mind off her. Then I wondered if she missed me while I was working, and she was alone in the house, probably not. I decided I was thinking too much and put on my jacket to cover my Glock after I put on the holster that I attached to my belt, and took Willy out to the Crown Vic. I uncovered the car and we got in, driving out and up to Buck's home. I decided to go bug him a while and see if he was hung over, even though he only drank Sprite. It's a psychological thing.

I drove up his drive and remembered where it all began with the classmate murders. How we ended up here partying with Buck's motorcycle friends and trying to avoid the killers. I was imagining all the people milling around the yard, just as Buck opened his front door and came out. I got out of the car and grabbed Willy's leash before he could take off.

"Hey, James, what's up?" He smiled at me.

"I took the day off and thought I'd come visit you for a while. I was bored at home; I guess I'm not much for sitting around if Penny's not there."

"Well, come on in, I was just cleaning house and I could use the company." Buck bent down and petted Willy as the pup was jumping around his feet. Willy liked Buck, they were both happy people and knew it. Buck picked up Willy, holding him up as Willy licked Buck's face, then we went into the house.

"I got some Pepsi in the fridge, help yourself. Heard anything about the movie yet." Buck asked as he put Willy down.

"Still too early, I haven't even signed the contracts yet. You'll be the first to know when it starts to roll. Trapper called me earlier that Earl Daws called him about getting out of the cop business and becoming a P.I., think we should bring him in on our firm?"

"Hey, Earl had some mysterious abilities that could come in handy. We could get Trapper to join too, make it a big company." Buck smiled.

"I told him that, he didn't say no." I opened my Pepsi and sat at the dining table where we had plotted our attack on the killers of the cheerleaders over a year ago. "A lot has happened since you and I used to drive around the car dealership. I hated that job even though it was a piece of cake to do. If I had a better car at the time I wouldn't have had a problem with the job. Winters here are way too miserable if you have to sit in a car for eleven hours without a heater."

"Maybe we could start our own security guard service like our old bosses did. A subsidiary of our detective business, I'd take care of that end of the business." He grinned at me as he was picking up his living room.

"It is something to think about. We had talked about doing that before I got my license. Now we could, you'd have to find places to guard."

"Hell, the way the economy is around here, most businesses would want to be guarded from the people trying to steal from them for the money. We'd make a fortune off of small businesses in strip malls." He was starting to think now.

My cell phone rang and I looked at the caller ID. It said private; I hated those calls, but thought it may be Drury with the contract. I answered, it was him.

"I'm out of the office now, but I could be there in an hour." I said in response to his question as to where I was. He agreed and I told Buck that I had to leave, the movie is rolling. He said good luck and I picked up Willy and went out to the car and headed to the office. It was money time.

*

Chapter 4

I got to the office with time to spare so I threw on a pot of coffee, I didn't know if they drank it but would have it ready. Have to please the money men. I straightened out the office a bit and had tied Willy's leash to the couch so he could rest there while I wheeled and dealed.

The men were punctual; they were there an hour from the time they called. Drury walked in with his henchmen and they took the chairs that they had the day earlier. Drury was smiling now, and seemed a bit more relaxed.

"Mr. Richards, we have the contracts and the check for you, so if you are ready we can proceed." He looked

Made for TV Murders

back to one of his men and the man opened the briefcase he carried and took out a manila envelope and handed it to Drury. He opened the envelope and took out a small stack of papers and laid them out on my desk, which I had cleared earlier just for this occasion. He was picking through them and pulled out a couple of pages and handed them to me and asked me to look them over. I did, I was satisfied with the terms written there and told him so.

"Great, Mr. Richards, let's proceed." He said.

I told him to please call me Jim, he said he would. He moved the papers to me and asked me to sign on a couple lines and one of his men would witness the signature. I looked to Drury and asked if the men were his assistants, he said no, they were company lawyers. I didn't want to aggravate the man by telling him I didn't like lawyers, so I held my tongue.

I had finished signing the papers he handed me and the lawyers signed their X on the papers. Drury smiled and shook my hand and thanked me for the honor to turn my book into a movie and handed me the check. I didn't want to be crass about it, so I just put it in my desk drawer so I could drool over it later.

"Who is going to be the director on this project?" I asked.

"We haven't officially approached a director yet but we are looking towards Betty Thomas as our first choice." He replied.

I knew her name as one of the stars on the old Hill Street Blues cop show and she had become a formidable director of many recent films. I told Drury of my approval on her selection if they could get her. He said they would be in talks.

"How long before this all goes into production?" I asked.

"It has already started, planning with the screenwriters has begun and I'm sure you'll approve, we are planning on filming the whole thing here in the Detroit area where it took place. There is a big move towards making films here and a number of new independent studios have been started that will accommodate our needs to film here. We have optioned a new movie studio in Detroit that will be our base of operations and you are more than welcome to come by and help out."

"I plan to do just that. I want to see this thing go along properly and with respect to the people who lived it. Please keep me informed as to when and where I go to do my part."

"I will shortly, as soon as we are more lodged into our new surroundings, I'll keep you apprised." He stood and his men jumped up and followed him out after they all said their good-byes. Willy was watching the whole show and then he put his head back down and closed his eyes.

Made for TV Murders

As soon as I was alone, I took the check out of the desk drawer and just stood staring at it. I was feeling light-headed and started dancing around the room. Willy stood up in surprise at my outburst and started yipping at me. I bent down and kissed him on the head and said I would buy him a ton of doggy treats. I sat at my desk chair and picked up the phone and called Penny's cell phone, but I got her voice mail. I looked at the clock and realized she was probably taping her show about now so left her a message that a certain handsome author wanted to have great sex with her tonight and hung up.

I took the check, and along with Willy, we went over to my bank and deposited the thing, knowing the IRS would be informed of the huge deposit. I didn't care; I paid all my taxes on every cent I took in including the finder's fee from the Bank of America for finding their embezzled money and the inheritance I received from Marty's estate. I didn't need aggravation from the government for not paying my fair share to them so they could screw up this country. I hated politicians more than I did lawyers.

I kept out a large portion of the deposit for spending money and stopped at a jewelry store and bought Penny a really nice diamond necklace and had it gift wrapped. Willy and I headed home in time to see Penny pulling into the drive. I let Willy loose and he ran to Penny and jumped around till she picked him up. I came up and kissed her hard and long.

"Are you going to be hanging around the house tonight?" she asked.

"Why?"

"I have a handsome author coming over tonight and I would appreciate it if you weren't here." she smirked.

I held up the package I got for her and her eyes went wide, but I kept it just out of reach from her and she followed me to the front door. We went in and she jumped on me taking the package from my hand. She tore into the wrapping and opened it and just stood staring at the thing. She asked if we had to wait until tonight for the great sex and then she latched on to me and dragged me to the bedroom.

We came out of the bedroom about two hours later, I was barely able to move, and plopped down on the couch.

"So are you feeling rich now?" Penny asked as she rubbed my thigh. I grabbed her hand before she could reach my private parts, the ones she attacked earlier. No sense in starting something all over again.

"No, but I feel relieved that I have enough cash to live comfortably for a long while, and to take care of your expensive tastes." I said.

"You'll never have enough money to take care of my desires." she laughed.

Made for TV Murders

"That's why I'm glad you have your own income from your show, when I'm broke, we're going to be living off your savings."

"Hell we are, that's for my old age, I plan for the future."

"Oh, so I could be broke and destitute and out on the street and you wouldn't lift a finger to help me?"

"No, so just be cautious with your income." she grinned at me.

"You do know that I have over a quarter million dollars in my bank account now? You aren't getting a cent from me; I'll put it in my will that it all goes to Willy and his doggy friends, leaving you out of the will."

"Meany, I'm withholding sex with you from now on. So don't even think about it."

I attacked her on the couch again and she didn't resist very hard.

We came up for air about thirty minutes later as my cell phone rang. I stretched my arm out over Penny so I could get the phone off the coffee table and looked at the caller ID, it said private. I debated on whether I would answer, but did. It was Trapper; he said he was waiting for me to call about my meeting with the studio people. I told him the deal was done and the whole thing was going to be filmed here in the area where it happened. He was quiet for a minute, then I heard him let out a tiny yippee, then he gathered himself and said he was glad for that. He could keep an eye on the production to make sure whoever portrayed him was accurate. I said I was sure they would bring in someone like Tom Selleck to play him; he was quiet again and said that would be nice. I laughed and told him I would talk to him tomorrow and hung up.

I thought about Buck, and I called him as I still lay next to Penny. I felt a bit embarrassed to be talking to Buck while Penny was naked next to me, but he couldn't see so I enjoyed the moment. He came on and I said he was going to be famous, the contracts were signed, he let out a yell and asked who was playing him. I said I didn't know but I would see if we could get Hulk Hogan to do the part. I could tell he was smiling, and he said he would appreciate that.

*

Chapter 5

After Penny and I made ourselves presentable, I called Deacon to let him know about the situation. He was ecstatic about the news and I could hear Lynn in the background cheering. He asked the same question everyone had asked so far, who was going to portray him. I said I didn't know, but we would try and find someone big and dumb to play the part. He laughed and said he would let that go until he saw me again. I feared for my life.

We talked a bit then hung up. "I seriously hope everyone isn't going to be disappointed with the choices of who plays who, it's a low budget movie and they may even select unknown actors to do the roles." I told Penny as she was making a sub sandwich for us to share. I helped cut up the foot long Italian bread, then she doled out the lunch meats on the bottom half and layered the meat and cheese like an expert. She cut the thing in half and I took mine and put mustard on it. She gave me a disgusted look and put Italian dressing on hers. We went to the couch again and ate our subs, downing it with a can of beer, or two.

We turned on the TV and watched a mini-series show about some woman who was trying to find her lost son in New York. It reminded me of my case out in New York and finding my missing stripper.

"Should I call Luther and tell him about the movie?" I asked Penny knowing that Luther and his motorcycle club was a big help during the classmate murders.

"I think they should know, after all the movie would be nothing without their help. Maybe they could actually be in the film, that's something to ask the producers," she said.

I looked at her and said, "I'm one of the producers, I hope. I don't know how much of a say I have in this venture but I will make waves if I'm ignored."

"Good, then you should call Luther and tell him." Penny said.

I went to the bedroom so Penny could continue watching TV, I called Buck and asked him if he had a phone number for Luther and explained that I wanted him and his friends to know about the movie, Buck said that was nice and went to get the number. I waited for a few minutes then Buck returned and gave me Luther's cell phone number. I thanked him and hung up. I dialed the number and waited till I heard a man's voice.

I asked if this was Luther and he said, "Who's asking?"

I was surprised by the question and said, "I'm Jim Richards."

"Damn man, how the hell are you." He yelled into the phone, causing me to move it away from my ear.

"I'm good, and I think you'll be good too." I said being cryptic.

"Okay, what does that mean?" He asked.

I told him about my book, which he already knew about and then I told him about the movie deal. He let out a yell causing me to move the phone again, and then he asked if they needed an experienced motorcycle gang to be in the film. I told him it was possible, but I couldn't say, the thing hadn't even been started yet, but I would see how they want to handle their part in the film.

"Well, brother, you keep me informed and I'll tell the guys about it."

I asked how everyone was and he said good, we talked a bit longer and then we finished. I went back out to Penny and filled her in on the people of her first fan club. She listened and laughed at the stories Luther told me.

We were too worn out from our rolling around earlier to do anything more tonight, but sleep. We cuddled in bed and talked about things we could do with our new wealth. I said that my book sales would also help with our funds, especially after the movie is aired. People will be curious about the details and it would help sell books, I hoped. I looked into Penny's eyes and told her I loved her and she said the same back. I asked her if she thought we could ever move out to Vegas like we kidded about and she said she liked the idea.

"You said you wanted to retire out there and maybe I could do my show from there. I don't know how my producer would take that, but I'd see if there's some way he could still be involved. He could come out with us and produce my show out there. I'll ask him tomorrow."

"Other than my family, the only friends we have here are Buck, Trapper and Becker and everyone else is out in Vegas. I know there would be enough crime for me to solve while out there too." I said.

"You mean to say you'd still do your P.I. work?" she looked at me like I was nuts.

"Well, maybe not as much, I'd still be busy writing all our adventures into books." I smiled. "Although, Earl Daws and Trapper said they were interested in a P.I. business, we could all go out there and set up an agency. There's more high profile crime out there than here. And Buck wants to start a security guard branch from our agency, something to think about too."

"Whatever, so long as you're happy and I'm with you. I'd be happy anywhere just as long as we are together." She kissed me on the nose and said she was sleepy and turned so we could spoon. She was asleep in minutes, I just laid there thinking.

Morning came fast and we were up getting ready for our day. Penny was taking Willy with her and I warned that she better let the pup have some time with the stage crew so he could maintain his macho attitude. She just shook her head and went to work. I went out to the car and stood looking at the covered Lincoln Town Car and said what the hell. I uncovered the Lincoln and drove it to work today; I wanted to play the part.

I took a slow drive to the office and just pulled into the parking lot as I saw Trapper walking towards the building. I honked the horn and he turned to see me. He gave me a big grin as I parked.

Made for TV Murders

"I hope this isn't all going to your head now, books, movies and mob limos." He said as he held the building door open for me. We went to my office and there were two men sitting on the chairs in the lobby. I greeted them and asked if they were here to see me, they said they were writers from the studio and they wanted to go over the script with me. I looked to Trapper and then back to them.

"You already have a script written?" I asked in wonder.

The younger of the two, I'd say about thirty and the other looked a bit older, said no, they had been working on it for a couple weeks, it was just a work in progress copy, more of an outline.

Trapper looked at me and said, "They were sure of themselves weren't they?"

I invited everyone in, and pointed to the extra chairs for the writers.

"Gentlemen, if I hadn't signed the contract till yesterday, why was there already a script being outlined?" I asked.

"Oh, the studio wanted to see a viable outline of the book and its transfer to screen before they went into signing you. Just to be sure it would work." Said the older man.

"And I presume it worked well for the screen?" I asked.

"Yes, they liked it, now we have to commit it to words, and rather quickly as they want to start filming in a couple of weeks."

"Oh, so there's no rush, eh?" I joked.

The younger man looked a bit upset, "Well, our jobs depend on it. This industry is fickle and we can be replaced by any number of writers who want our jobs. So I hope you can help us, being as you are a writer and know the story."

Trapper was smiling from his chair by the door; I looked at him and pointed my finger, silently saying to shut up. I asked for the outline to read it before we started anything and the older man handed it to me. I sat back and started to read. The room was quiet for about fifteen minutes as I read, which surprised me as Trapper didn't interject a smart-alec remark and then I stopped half way through and put the papers down.

I looked at the men and asked them for their names, the older one said, Harry and the younger said Todd. Harry and Todd, I thought about that and then asked if they even read my book?

"Oh, yes, I loved it." Exclaimed Todd the younger.

"And you wrote this from my book?" Pointing to the script.

"We had specific guidelines about how to proceed on it. We just followed those and the studio heads liked it." Harry the older said.

I looked at Trapper and said the studio turned me into a thirty-five year old hunk. Trapper burst out laughing.

*

Chapter 6

"Don't laugh, you're a broken down drunk, just barely holding on to your badge only because you can hide your alcohol problem." I smiled at Trapper who went silent. He stood and came to my desk and picked up the papers, then went back to his chair and read it.

"You S.O.B., it doesn't say that. But you are a handsome thirty-five year old hunk. Penny is a thirty-two year old virgin." He was laughing his head off. "Okay, not a virgin, but this is a pile of crap. No offense guys, I'm sure you are just doing what you were told." He smiled and threw the papers back on the desk.

Harry the older looked distressed, "I'm really sorry, but that was in the guidelines we received from the studio. They have demographics to conform to, hitting the 18 to 40 year old market. It sells better to the network."

Bob Moats

"Do you realize that the baby-boomers out in the world are all now hitting their 60's and they make up a big part of the population?" I offered.

"Until they all die out." Trapper threw in. I gave him a dirty look and said he could go sooner than that.

Todd the younger said, "I know that, but the networks aim their commercials towards the younger crowd."

"Okay, so why do I see so many commercials for Viagra, Depends, Metamucil and all those drug commercials running every twenty minutes? Those are aimed at us old folk." I countered.

"Yes, you're right. But in certain time slots, they are. Big Show is aiming for the prime time early viewing, the younger crowd." Harry offered.

"Okay, if this were a fictional story, I would say let's make me a handsome stud, but this is based on a real life incident, a true crime story that shouldn't be played with. All the people involved were real and featured on national television when the crime first occurred. People saw us and know us. You come along and re-write the story and people aren't going to be happy, me for one."

Harry and Todd were silent, not knowing what to do. They must have been new to this business, having been thrown into writing something that has a history.

Made for TV Murders

"Look guys, give me a few names of people who fed you this drivel and I'll raise a stink. We'll get this back on the right track and we can write it in quick time. Okay?" I said.

Harry looked flustered and gave me a name, Howard Martin, head of Really Big Show Pictures, and a number when I asked. I dialed the number and got a secretary, who transferred me around a few times before I got Howard Martin's personal secretary.

"Mr. Martin is in conference at the moment, may I take a message?" she asked.

"Only if he returns it. I'm Jim Richards, the author of the Classmate Murders and one of the producers of the movie being made of said book. He better return my call about this crappy script outline I was given, as soon as possible."

"I'll pass it along to Mr. Martin, sir. He should be finished in a half hour." she said.

"If I don't hear from him in forty minutes, then I'm calling back and I won't be happy." I hung up.

Harry and Todd went a bit wide-eyed and said nothing; Trapper was chuckling from his chair and said how delightful it was to observe the process of film making. I flipped him a quick finger and then looked to the two writers squirming in their chairs.

"You guys are new to this aren't you?" I asked.

Harry grinned, "Is it that obvious?"

"Yes, well, you both are not the arrogant, self-serving writers that I have seen in films or was that script writing for the demographics, too?"

"Actually, most screenwriters are a bit arrogant and self-serving." Todd the younger offered. "Harry and I just started writing for this production, our first job. I hate to say it, because we came cheap. This is not going to be a big budget film, sorry."

I offered coffee and they took it, then Trapper moved over to my desk and started reading the outline again.

"Damn, the ending has you and Buck in a shoot out with Alice Stone, where was my part in it. For crying out loud, you and Buck had your hands in the air when I came in and shot her!" He was incensed.

He read as the rest of us sat until my phone rang thirty-five minutes after my call. "Hello?"

"Mr. Richards, Howard Martin here, it's so good to finally come in contact with you. Drury said you were a pleasure to deal with. I've heard so much about you."

"I deny everything they said." I waited for him to understand I was kidding, but he didn't respond. "I'm calling about this putrid attempt to retell my story on the classmate murders. It's turned into a piece of fiction, not a word of truth."

Made for TV Murders

Martin was silent for a minute then said, "May I call you Jim?" he asked, I said he could. "Jim, you shouldn't have gotten that outline without my talking to you first. I'm sorry they sprung it on you. Please understand that outline is just our way of getting the network on board with our film, we had to placate them so we could get the green light. I hope you understand, your story will be told as you so aptly wrote it in your book. I read it, it was very good."

I thanked him and felt a bit better now hearing this, "So, am I to work with Harry and Todd to get a good working script to you?"

"Yes, please do, and tell Harry and Todd to behave, they are on a short leash until they can show they have the right stuff. Are we good now?" he asked.

"I feel a bit better, yes. I was not happy to see my book being changed around, you can't change the truth."

"Well, it can be bent a little, otherwise how would we know exactly what Abe Lincoln said when he went to the Ford Theatre that fateful night. We have to embellish a little to make it seem real. As Doug Henning once said, it's all an illusion."

I didn't feel like arguing a point made by a now deceased magician, but let it go. I just wanted to be assured I could make this right and tell the story as it happened.

"Well, I'll get working with your men and we'll have something for you shortly." I said.

"Great, fantastic. I'll look forward to reading what you guys hash out. I also look forward to meeting with you and Penny, your wife. I have seen her TV show on numerous occasions and must say you are a lucky man. How has she responded to our little film?"

"Well, Penny takes everything with a grain of salt. She wasn't real crazy about it in the beginning but she came around and even joked about having Jaclyn Smith portray her. Do you have any ideas on which actors are in line for the roles?"

"Well, we have central casting starting to put together a list of actors available and we have put out casting calls in Variety and the other trade papers. We are already getting some response. I'll give you a call when we go into auditions and you can be in on the process. After all, you have a producing credit to live up to, may as well get some mileage out of it." I could tell he was grinning on his end, I was just hoping he was serious.

"How about a director. I've done a bit of theatre work, stage mostly, and I know that the director can make or break a production." I said.

"How right you are, they are the cornerstone of any film, if they crumble, the building would fall. Glad you have a bit of knowledge of the process, it helps. We have been in talks with a couple of directors, none to mention right now but we feel confident that we will find the right one. I hope you will be in on the process also in selecting the director." he said.

"I'd like that very much; I want to work with him to bring the reality of the crime as it happened. I did live it and suffered through it. I can bring that to the director."

"And to the script. I hope this venture will be fruitful for all, I feel good about it. Thanks so much for this talk and look forward to many more, perhaps over a beer or two?"

I was now liking him more, "Well, you know how to push my buttons. I do want to see this movie succeed and be something that the people who lived it can be proud of. And something that can be noticed at Emmy time." I said as I grinned.

"Ah, you are already starting to sound like a producer. Well, get me a script that will knock my socks off and we'll celebrate." then we finished and hung up.

I looked to Harry and Todd, and said, 'We got our work cut out for us."

*

Chapter 7

Trapper said he had to go do some real criminal investigating and said to make him look good in the script. I asked what was wrong with the broken down drunk scenario, he flipped me the bird and left. I looked to Todd and Harry and they just sat smiling at me. It was a bit unnerving the way they had that puppy dog look in their eyes, like waiting for me to throw them a bone.

"Okay, guys, we need to take the book point by point, outline the actual story and then flesh it out. Does that work for you?" I asked.

They both just nodded their heads and kept smiling. "Guys, take something to write on and let's get moving."

The reached down and opened their briefcases, took out pads and pencils and placed them on my desk. I guess they were going to do this the old fashion way, write it out by hand. I pulled over the small table that my laptop sat on and turned it on to go to my book outline of the classmate murders. I told the guys to hang for a minute while I got my head back into the story. I skimmed the thing and then opened my desk drawer and took out a copy of my book and put it in front of them.

Made for TV Murders

"Okay, let's pound this thing out." I said.

We spent the better part of four hours writing and re-writing a script and we managed to get just past the murder of Joyce Harper in her office from poison. This was the first visual appearance of Trapper as a main character; I owed it to him to make him look good. This was also where Barry Becker had a small part in the story till later and I knew it would make him happy to see his inclusion. Back when I had been writing my book I sat with Trapper about what happened at Joyce's office, since I wasn't there after the murder, and he told me what happened to the best of his recollection, just so my story would be somewhat accurate.

We broke for lunch and I took them to a nearby Subway in the limo, they loved it, and we had our meal while still talking about the script. We went back to the office and I called Penny to see if she was home and tell her about my day.

"They tried to make you a hunk, that's hilarious." she said.

"Hey, I'm ruggedly handsome, in a hunk sort of way." I defended myself.

"Yes, you are rugged. Like the Rocky Mountains. But you'll always be my hunk." She laughed and hung up. I would remind her later about that statement.

The boys and I got back to writing, I was plugging it into my laptop and they scribbled on their pads of

46

paper. We now got to the part where Penny and her show's guest were almost killed by the light beam in her studio and I was looking at the clock on my wall. It was now about five-twenty and I was wearing down from thinking and typing. Even back when I wrote my book, I only worked on a chapter each day, then I would polish it the next day when my mind was fresh. Besides, Howard said we had a week before they really wanted to get into production.

"Guys, where are you staying out here?" I asked.

Harry spoke first, "We're in a Red Roof Inn over in a town called Roseville."

"Yeah, I know the place. Well, I think we need to call it a day and start fresh tomorrow morning, sound good to you?" I asked.

They both looked tired and agreed to the rest. I said they could leave everything here, it would be safe. They shook my hand and left. I sat back down for a minute and looked to the start of the script on my laptop. I made a copy of it on my flashdrive and then I hit the print button and the pages came out of the laser printer, then I gathered them up and put them in a manila envelope and headed home.

I realized that I hadn't seen Penny's show today, so I wasn't sure if there was anything to worry about when I got home.

Made for TV Murders

I drove along Jefferson Avenue taking the long way home so I could enjoy the limo and the stares from people in cars wondering who the celebrity could be. Unfortunately, they were straining to see the back of the car for the celebs; I was just the lowly driver. The car had the limo tint windows so it was hard to see in the back, I thought about getting one of those blow up dolls and put her back there to make it feel right as I drove.

I got to our drive and found about six cars in the drive and off the side on the lawn. I had to drive out around them to get to my parking space. I was wondering what I was going to walk into. I put the car cover on the Lincoln and went to the front door, Penny didn't open up for me like she usually does, I went in gritting my teeth.

I walked into a room full of angry looking women, my blood chilled and I held my breath. Penny saw me and came over to introduce me to the angry women. They just kind of snarled their hellos and Penny excused us to go out into the kitchen.

"What the hell was that?" I said quietly, afraid they would hear me.

"I had a local group of women on my show today that had formed their own "First Wives Club"," she smiled at me weakly.

"Okay, how did they end up here and are they dangerous?" I asked fearing for my private parts.

"I may have mentioned that we could continue our talk here and before I realized what I had said, they all were heading for their cars to follow me." Her smile turned a little downward.

"What do they expect from you as their new leader?"

"Well, remember you are my fourth husband, so I have a little experience in these matters." She was smirking now, like it was a badge of honor to have so many ex-husbands in her past.

I stared a bit then said, "Let's see, your first husband had an affair with an intern at his company and later married her, then she took him for everything he had when he had an affair with another intern, he was a company man wasn't he?" She whacked my arm. "Your second husband died of a heart attack, rest his soul, probably from your sexual attacks. Oh, wait he died in the bed of another woman, didn't he?" Penny whacked my arm again. "Your third husband finally decided he wasn't sure if he liked men or women, but the men won out, and you got all his dresses in the divorce." She whacked me again, as I was now finding the humor in it all.

"You are a pig." She smiled at me.

"Is that what you're telling the Mongolian warriors out there?"

"No, I bragged about you, they all admire me for having such a good husband."

Made for TV Murders

"Is that why they all greeted me with blood in their eyes?"

"No, you came in just when Margaret was talking about her cheating husband. They were getting a little worked up." Penny said as I went to the fridge.

I took out a can of Pepsi and smiled, saying, "Have fun with your little friends, play nice. I'm going to my office to work on my screen play." I kissed her on the nose and went off to the porch. I had put in the corner of the porch a computer desk, and set up a place to work on my books, that way I could see outside on nice days, rare for Michigan, and I could watch Penny swing around her stripper pole to work off her tensions. I inserted the flashdrive in the new laptop I bought for my home office and woke the computer from its sleep. I opened up my writing program, NoteTab 6, and brought up the file of what the boys and I wrote today. I stared at the thing and thought a while on it.

About a half hour later, and two more pages of writing, Penny came in and announced that all the women had vacated the premises. I smiled and asked when the next meeting was. She said there would be no more here; she hoped they respected her privacy. I wondered if we wouldn't get calls in the middle of the night for support from my now expert divorce leader. I handed her the printouts from earlier and she went to the porch glider to read. She was swinging slowly causing the glider to do its annoying squeals, so I asked her to move to the easy chair, she gave me a frown and did.

She finished and came back to me and said it sounded good so far, then she asked if I was going to put all the steamy sex we had in the script? I said I was going to make me look like a hot Latin lover. She laughed out loud and went into the kitchen. I could still hear her laughing her head off. Just wait till later tonight in bed, I'd show her who was a hot Latin lover.

*

Chapter 8

Penny and I were camped out on the couch with our refreshments and snacks, watching TV and I was scratching Willy's belly as he lay on his back next to me. He snorted and sighed and looked contented, Penny was munching on chips and looking contented. We were a contented family.

My cell phone rang and I debated whether to answer, Penny said to do it. I did. It was Buck asking how the movie was progressing. I told him and we talked for a bit then he asked if we had any cases to handle.

"I'm closing down shop for a while until I see how this goes with the film. Why don't you go out and visit Maria in Vegas for a while?" I said.

Made for TV Murders

"Hell no, I want to see if the Hulkster gets my part and comes into town." He was excited.

"Well, things can change, so don't be disappointed." I warned. "I'll let you know what is going on as I find out." We said our good-byes and hung up.

"You know, I think I will be happy when this gets moving, so everyone will stop asking me who is going to play them."

Penny looked at me and said, "About that, who is going to play my part?"

I gave her a dirty look and went off to the bed room, yelling Fernando the hot Latin lover will be open for business.

She yelled, "You'll be out of business soon enough. Lack of customers and faulty equipment."

I plopped down on the bed and flipped on the TV in the bedroom, and went to Showtime to see if they had a good sex flick on. They had a movie about three animals traveling across the country trying to find their home. Oh well.

Penny came in wrapped in the blanket off the couch. She stood by the door giving me a sexy look and said with a poor Spanish accent, "Hello, Fernando, you like to play with Tina Marie?" She brought a leg out of the blanket and I could tell she was not dressed.

Bob Moats

I flipped the TV off and said in an even poorer Spanish accent, "Come to me my little desert cactus." Penny started to laugh; I corrected myself, "my little shot of tequila... my little Mexican taco... my little Chihuahua." Penny was breaking up now and threw off the blanket and jumped on me.

Okay, a hot Latin lover I was not. But we did well enough to work up a sweat.

Next morning we did our start of the day ritual and headed off to our jobs. I got to the office and found Todd and Harry sitting in the lobby. I waved them to follow and we went into the office and resumed our positions like we had never left. I showed them a few new pages that I had worked out at home and they liked the new lines. We worked from there and about two hours later we paused to act out the script so we could see what we had for time. We read through the script playing parts and reading actions, we came up with about an hour and a half of running time. This pleased the two men as we had four hours to fill and we barely touched on half the book.

The next four days whizzed by and we had a finished script. I called Howard Martin and told him, he asked if I could email the PDF of the script and I said that could be arranged. He gave me his private email address and I wrote it down. He said he'd call after he read it and had a few of his people go over it. He thanked me for my help with the script and we finished our call. I looked to Harry and Todd as they just sat smiling like two Cheshire cats.

Made for TV Murders

"Okay guys, I guess we're finished here till I hear back from Howard, so what are you going to do now?" I asked.

Harry spoke first, "We'll have to hang around until Howard does call with his changes, then we have to fix the things he doesn't like and basically start over. It's the nature of the beast."

"Yeah, well it's not my nature, that script was perfect for what happened back then and I'll be damned if they change anything, I guess we'll see what happens. Enjoy the area and I'll call you when I hear something."

The two tired writers left and I sat turning the text file of the script into a PDF file and emailed it to Howard. I ran off a couple copies on the printer and put them together in folders so I could show Penny and get her opinion. She maybe goofy acting most the time but she had a razor sharp mind and a good sense of what worked and what didn't.

It was now about four-thirty and I decided there was not much more to do here, so I packed up everything and was about to leave when I found a young woman standing just outside my door. She looked flustered and I asked if she were lost.

"No, I'm looking for Jim Richards, the private detective." She spoke softly as though someone may hear her. I just barely did and told her I was him. "I'm Celeste Davis, I need your help Mr. Richards, I have a problem." I invited her in to the office and said to have a seat.

"Now Celeste, what is it you need?" I asked.

"I'm afraid for my life, I'm being stalked and harassed by a man I hardly know." She seemed embarrassed to talk.

"Please, don't be afraid to talk to me, I've heard it all." I said in a light voice hoping to make her more at ease.

"I met a man at a bar in Warren and we... well, we had a night together and I thought it was over, but he started to call and come by and I don't really want to have anything to do with him. After the first night I found I didn't really like him but he's getting insistent."

"Did you tell the police?"

"Yes, but they won't do anything unless he gets violent or hurts me. It's stupid for them to wait till he does me harm before they even help."

"Where do you live?" I asked.

"In Warren, just off 13 Mile and Hoover."

I thought about calling Trapper and asking for his take on it, it wasn't in his jurisdiction, but maybe he could help.

Made for TV Murders

"Give me a minute." I said as I took out my cell phone. After about three rings he came on.

"So, who is playing me?" Was the first thing he said as he answered.

"I have no idea, we just finished the script today and it needs approval, then they will go for casting, be patient. Now I have a problem I need some professional cop advice, do you have a minute?"

"Okay, give." I loved his brevity. I told him about the girl in my office and her problem and he said, "it's a sad fact that police can't do much unless there is a serious threat or an attempt, it's a catch 22 situation, a person wants protection, but cops can't do much unless the person gets beat-up or murdered. I wish we had the time and man power to help these people. Maybe something for Buck to do, watch your client."

"Yeah, maybe I'll talk to him about it; just keep in mind what I told you, in case of problems." He agreed and we hung up.

"Celeste, I can have an associate watch you for a few days and see what your stalker does. Can you afford my fee?" I could see that she wasn't in the dough, but I wasn't worried about being paid, I just wanted this girl to feel safe.

"Mr. Richards, I have a small IRA that I can cash, I'm not rich and my job is minimum wage, I'll try to pay you, maybe in installments." She looked so sad; I couldn't let her hang any longer.

"Celeste, don't worry about the fee, I do occasionally help people Pro-Bono when I feel it's worth it. I'll have my associate get in touch with you today and we'll see what we can do to help you. Understand though, we can only do so much that the law allows, but sometimes we can just have a talk with your stalker, sort of let him know it would be in his best interest to leave you alone. But sometimes that back-fires, so we have to be careful. I need any information you have on this guy so we can check his background." I handed her my pad and pencil and asked her to write as much as she knew about him.

She wrote a couple of lines and then added her contact information when I asked.

"Okay, Celeste, I'll have my partner call, his name is Buck Carson, but I'd advise laying low till he calls. Is that all right for you?"

She agreed and we stood, I shook her hand gently and took her to the door. We said good-bye and she went off. I went back to my desk and called Buck.

"Jimmy, has the Hulkster agreed to play me yet." he said with a grin in his voice.

I was ready to scream, but held it, "No, Buck, I'll let you and everyone else know when we have a cast, so till then, stop asking!"

"You got it chief, what's up?" he asked.

"I got a Pro-Bono case of a young girl who's being stalked by a one-night stand. She's fearful for her life, cops can't help, you got a few days to devote to protecting her and maybe scaring the stalker off? I'll pay you for the time."

"Oh hell, I got nothing better to do, love to help her out. Keep the pay, I just need something to do to take my mind off the damn movie." He said sounding happy to be back on the job.

"Okay, got a pen and I'll give you her information. I'm going to call Trapper to see if I can get some background on the freak, I'll pass on what I find to you." I gave him the info and he said he'd call the girl as soon as we finished. I thanked him and said to be careful.

*

Chapter 9

I re-dialed Trapper, and he came on, "I was wondering when you would get back to me to do a check on your stalker." He said sounding smug.

I laughed, "I guess you know me well enough. Maybe I can get a computer link hooked to your system, then I can do my own checks."

"I don't think the big bosses would like that. Give me what you got on him and I'll see what I can do to help the girl. I felt a little bad about the fact that our hands are tied, so give me the info."

I read the information Celeste had written, the guy's name was Steve Nelson, and Trapper said to give him a couple hours to see what he comes up with. I thanked him and we hung up. I suddenly remembered that I was just heading out when Celeste came by, I was glad that there would be a break from the last few days, now that we had a case, even if it was for free.

I headed home thinking about the script and wondering how they could change it. The thing ran about three and a half hours, allowing for commercials to make it a four hour show, and it was complete and had a good thread through it. I didn't like the idea of changing it to please some idiot who had no idea of what went on back then. If they didn't like it, I would make my own damn film and sell it to cable. I suddenly realized I was in my driveway; I must have driven on auto pilot. I noticed there was a Jeep in the drive; I wondered if Penny was entertaining a man, I said "nah" to myself. I got out and up to the door and went in.

I was a bit shocked by the sight of Penny laying prone, face-down on a portable table, naked save for a towel across her great butt, being massaged by a rather good looking, tanned, blond woman. Penny looked up to me, smiled and said to get in line.

Made for TV Murders

"I have… uh... a little work to do in my office... you just go on with your... um... massage." I stammered and then zipped out to the porch. I had flashbacks to the strip club in Vegas when Penny was being hit on by Tiffany, the bi-sexual dancer. Penny refused to do a three way with Tiffany and me, but she made up for it in many other ways. I was now relishing in the sight of that woman rubbing down Penny and had to adjust my pants. A few minutes later, Penny came waltzing out to the porch all oiled up with just the towel around her. My pants needed adjusting again.

"Hi sweetie, have a good day writing?" She asked as she planted a kiss on the top of my bald head. I was just staring at her great legs and said I did.

"Was that part of your show today?" I asked while I shifted in my chair to help get my pants to adjust again.

"Yes, Lynda came by to talk about massages and how they help tone and relax a person. I hired her to come here and give me the full treatment. You want a massage too? I asked her to wait." She smiled at me. I was a bit amazed that she would let an attractive woman rub my body all over, I almost accepted, but then thought it may be a trap.

"Well, that would be nice; I think I'll wait for you to give me a body rub later. Thanks anyways." I smiled.

"Okay, your loss, I'll tell her she can pack up and go." She turned and the towel flew open enough for me to see her cute naked butt, I adjusted again.

About a half hour later, Penny came back in with just a robe on and pulled a chair over to my desk. She plopped her elbows on the desk and cradled her cute face in her hands.

"So tell me, how goes the progress of the movie and how was your day?" She mumbled through her hands.

"The script is finished, well, it's finished by us, but they have to approve it first and then force me to make changes. I'll go down fighting before I change it. I'll pull out of the thing if they screw with it."

"You'd have to give back all that money," she said.

I looked at her for a minute and then said, "Okay, I'll stay on, but I won't like it." She just smiled at that.

"I also took on a case of protection for a young girl who had a one-night stand with a would be stalker." I explained the meeting today with Celeste and that I was doing it for free.

"A freebie? Was she cute? Did she give you a full body massage?" She was poking my ribs now.

"Stop that, and no she didn't do anything to me but look frightened. I do good things for people when they need it. Remember Marsha Webster during the mistress murder, I didn't charge for that case."

Made for TV Murders

"Sure, but you made one hundred and thirty thousand dollars by tracking down her embezzled funds from the bank. Did you forget that?" she countered.

"Okay, so I did get paid for it, but I didn't start out charging anything. What do you want from me, I try to do nice things."

"Sweetie, I love you for that, and a few other things." She let the robe open a bit and winked at me. "That massage stimulated a few parts of my body that need tending to that Lynda couldn't provide, you know what I mean?" She smiled and went off into the other room. I adjusted my pants again and followed her.

About an hour and a half later, we were back on the couch again; this was getting to be a habit. We sat watching "CSI" the original, I didn't like the Miami version, New York was all right. Since I became an investigator, I've watched a few real CSI and CSU teams, including a plain old forensic team from the Michigan State Police and they didn't have the glamour that they had on TV. I thought about my script and wondered if it should be Hollywoodized, just to make it more glamorous. Most shows I watch on TV go for the adventure and excitement rather than a good plot. Don't get me wrong, there are a good number of shows with great plots, but they all get canceled in their first season. At least my movie can't be canceled, it's only one show.

"This is stupid; the crooks are getting away in their car, why didn't the cops shoot the tires on the car to slow him down." Penny yelled at the TV. I smiled.

"Because it would make the plot end sooner, they have to have a chase and shooting the tires, it's not something they would do, and yes it's stupid." I answered.

"Okay, you have to start writing scripts for these shows; you'd make them more exciting." She kissed me on the cheek. I changed the subject.

"I have to admit, your body was well toned, I think you should have a massage more often." I said as Penny munched on chips.

"You only want to watch one woman rub oil all over another woman, you can't fool me." She spit a few chip crumbs as she spoke. I brushed them off me to the couch where Willy gladly licked them up.

My cell phone rang in time to avoid Penny's accusations of my ogling her masseuse. It was Buck; I answered and asked if he got hold of Celeste.

"Yep, she's a real nice girl. We are getting along fine. Heard from Trapper yet on the stalker?" He asked.

"No, it's kind of strange that he hasn't gotten back to me yet, maybe he couldn't find anything on the guy. Play it by ear and if the guy comes around, just look threatening, don't rough him up, we don't need a lawsuit, or having to bail you out of jail."

"I'll know how to handle it, I won't cause any trouble, just let him know I'm around. Maybe I'll tell him I'm her husband and if he keeps coming around, I'll pound him into the ground." He laughed.

I thought that may actually work, one look at Buck and he wouldn't be coming back. "As soon as I hear from Trapper I'll call."

We finished and hung up. I told Penny what Buck said and we watched the rest of the show on TV. About an hour later my cell rang again and the caller ID came up with just a number, the area code was Los Angeles.

"Hello." I said.

"Jim baby, Howard here, I read the script and I loved it! I had my people read it with me and we are all excited, I tell ya excited. We are starting to narrow down a director, I'll email you a list and you can look them over, give your feedback, but the studio may want someone they know, so we'll wait and see. Anyway, love the script and tell Harry and Todd to hang in for us to come out to start filming. I got my production advance man and a location manager heading out there, they'll call you when they arrive and you can show them all the places where the crime happened. This is going to be great, we'll talk later, take care, baby." and he hung up. Amazing, I didn't say a word.

I played the recording that my Palm Treo cell phone makes of every call that comes in or goes out on the phone, so Penny could hear what he said and she smiled, saying we were going to be famous.

*

Chapter 10

The next morning broke with storms outside. Michigan weather was a pain for weather forecasters to predict, it changed so much and so fast. I never believed weather forecasters anyway, they were usually wrong. This morning I was forcing myself to get going, Penny had already left for her studio, but before she left, she was grumbling about the weather and asked me what it was like today in Vegas. I chuckled and looked to the computer for the national weather site; it was sunny and hot in Vegas. Oh well.

I thought about calling Trapper to see if he came up with anything on our stalker, but I knew he'd call if he had something. I really wasn't planning on going into the office today, so Penny left Willy with me and he was sitting on the floor looking sad. I knew that look, he was hungry. I went to the kitchen and poured him a bowl of the crap that dogs eat. I took one of the tiny bits and smelled it, then put it back. It wasn't very appetizing.

Made for TV Murders

I was debating if I wanted to eat breakfast when my cell phone rang from out in the family room. I ran to it, stubbing my toe on one of the snack bar stools and swore out loud. I hopped to the phone and saw it was Trapper.

"About time you called. What have you got?" I yelled into the phone while rubbing my toe.

"I got zip. This guy is either a spook for the Feds, or he has laid so low he doesn't blip on any of my checks. Nada. Sorry but he just has no past or present." Trapper sounded at a loss.

"He has no driver's license? Nothing?" I asked.

"Not that I can find, are you sure this girl gave you his correct name?"

"Well, it's possible he gave her false info, so she couldn't have him tracked. That's a thought." I offered.

"Yeah, he's probably married and screwing around, no need to give out a real name to blow his cover."

"I'll call Buck and see what he can come up with. Oh, and to keep you informed, the script for the movie has been approved, if you want to see a copy of it, you'll just have to come by to read it." He said he would and we hung up.

About thirty seconds later someone was knocking at my door, it was Trapper.

"Damn it, I wish everyone would stop doing that." I exclaimed.

"What, calling you from your driveway, it's fun," he said as he shook off the rain from his overcoat. "Where's the script and I better look good in it." He smiled and took the papers I held out for him. I told him to go sit and read, it would take him a while to do so. He sat and started to read as I went back to the kitchen followed by Willy, and toasted a muffin.

About an hour later, Trapper put the paper down and looked to me sitting on the couch, "This is good, real good. Thank you for my part."

"You're done already?" I said amazed he had finished it so quickly.

"I took a speed reading course years ago, police work is mostly tons of paperwork." He said.

"So you think it will work?" I asked.

"Well, it depends on who plays me." He smiled at me and I gave him the finger.

My cell phone rang and it was Buck, "Good morning, and where did you sleep?"

He laughed, "I slept on the couch, it was a quiet night. No problems. Any word from Trapper."

"As a matter of fact he is sitting here and says there was no info on Steve Nelson, or whatever his name is. Put Celeste on the phone." I asked.

Celeste came on and I asked, "Celeste, did Steve give you any other info about him, we can't find him under the info you gave me."

"He talked very little about himself; just his name and he lived in Sterling Heights. He said he was a financial advisor, everything I wrote down for you yesterday. That's all he shared."

"Okay, just sit tight and let Buck do his job. Listen to him; he has your best interest in mind. Put Buck back on the phone, please." I said I'd talk later and Buck came back on.

"So, we have no idea what this guy is capable of?" He said.

"Nope, so be vigilant, and don't get killed." I laughed and we finished.

"I guess we don't do much now till he shows up and I hope Buck proceeds with caution." I said.

"I'll give a friend of mine in the Warren PD a call and let him know what's up." Trapper said as he thumbed through the script.

"Do you have friends on every police force in Macomb and Wayne County?" I wondered.

"It's a network, we are all connected through a local gathering place," he paused, "It's a very nice bar in my jurisdiction. That way I can arrest anyone who gets carried away." He laughed and skimmed the script again.

"I didn't notice very many heavy sex scenes between you and Penny in this thing." He looked at me and grinned. "I seem to remember Deacon telling me you guys were always in Penny's bedroom rolling around."

"Wouldn't you like to know?"

Trapper stood and looked out the front window, it had stopped raining, "Well, time to go back to work, the criminals will be on the streets now. Keep me informed on the movie and the stalker. I'll call my friend to let him know about it."

He went out and I was alone in the house again. I couldn't go bug Buck, he was working. I looked at Willy and said we may as well go to my office; at least I can concentrate there.

I gathered Willy and we went out to the Crown Vic, I didn't know if it would rain again, so I didn't use the limo. We drove to the office and went in, I set Willy down and turned on the TV and switched to the Cartoon Network. Willy was sniffing around and I pulled my laptop to my desk and opened up the new story I was writing about the Showgirl murders. I could at least write if I had nothing better to do. Hell, maybe they'd make it into a movie too.

I putzed, typing for about an hour and a half when my cell rang, it was Trapper. I answered and said hello.

"I called my friend, John Handley, over in Warren and told him about your girl, he said he'd watch for any news coming in on her or Buck and call me. That's about all that we can do right now, I'll let you know. Can't talk, my captain is skulking the squad; he's bored so he comes in to bother us, later." He said and hung up.

I looked at Willy lying on the couch sleeping peacefully, I got up and went to lie down next to him, he didn't like that. I was just starting to nod off when my cell phone rang again; I had it in my pocket so I wouldn't have to get up. Caller ID came up with just numbers, but I answered anyways.

"Mr. Richards, this is Scott Bailey, production manager for Big Show, I'm in town now with the location manager, can we meet?"

"Sure, where are you?" I asked still groggy from almost dozing off.

"Well, Bill and I are in a motel just off a road called Little Mack by Masonic, it's a Comfort Inn. Harry Gates, the writer, recommended it. He's actually at the Red Roof Inn, but they are full up, so we came down the road to this place."

"I know the place, I can meet you there, what room are you in?" I asked.

"Ground floor, front, room 16. We'll be waiting to talk, thanks." He hung up and I wondered if most people just thought that other people didn't mind being hung up on.

I decided to take the limo; I wanted to look the part. It was still at the house but it was just a short drive to get it, and I put Willy in the kitchen with the board up so he couldn't get in any trouble in the house. He didn't like it.

As I drove over thinking about all the places that the crime had happened in and around the area, I figured we'd start at Buck's because a lot of it happened there. I called Buck to warn him that we may be going to his place; he said he figured that so he and Celeste were already at his place and making it all nice and clean for us. I asked him if Celeste was all right with the change, he said she offered to help him clean up and she was intrigued by the fact that a Hollywood movie would be made there.

I arrived at the Comfort Inn and pulled up to the front of the building as close to room 16 as possible that would accommodate the extra length of the limo. It wasn't a full stretch limo but a shorter version, one I could comfortably drive and not look like a chauffeur. I went to the door and knocked, the door opened.

Made for TV Murders

"Mr. Richards, welcome, come on in." A rather tan, tall man spoke. He looked like the west coast image I had of Hollywood types, he just didn't have a cardigan sweater tied around his neck. "I'm Scott Bailey and this is Bill Urban." He pointed to his partner in the room. "Howard said to depend on you for the places that the crime happened, so we are ready to start scouting out locations."

"Well, I have a few places we can visit today if that's acceptable with you." I said.

"Great, we're pressed for time and we will also need to go to the studio location that the production team will be working out of and would appreciate it if you could help us locate the studio."

I said I would do that and asked for the address, he gave it to me as I pulled out my Palm TX and brought up the map program. I entered the address and the program pinpointed the location. It was just below Eight Mile Road in Detroit, fairly close to where Earl Daws was fighting crime. I thought about calling Earl to let him know we would be playing in his backyard.

*

Chapter 11

They were impressed that the limo was mine and got into the back. I had the privacy window down so I could talk to them as they lounged in the comfortable seats and told them a little about the origin of the limo. They were impressed that it was a former mob limo.

"You haven't rented a vehicle yet, have you?" I asked.

"No, Harry and Todd met us at Metropolitan Airport and drove us to the Motel. If you could later, take us to rent a car, I'd appreciate it." Bill said.

"No problem, so how is the production shaping up."

"Well, they are starting to cast the bit players and have narrowed the director down to two people, both experienced in crime dramas. One of them has even won an Emmy for his direction, but he probably would ask for more than we can afford to pay. So they probably will go with the second choice, Wayne Barrack."

I never heard of him and I loved to watch credits on movies and television, hadn't seen the name. The two men were discussing and looking over some papers they brought in a large envelope, so I just drove quietly. We arrived at Bucks, he and Celeste came out as we pulled up. Celeste sat on a lawn chair on the porch and Buck came to us. I introduced Buck and Scott laughed.

Made for TV Murders

"I'm sorry Mr. Carson, I had read the book and the script and I pictured you just as you are." he said.

Buck told both men to call him Buck and said no problem, he like the way I had written him in the book. He asked us to come to the picnic table he had brought from the back and we could talk about the property and what went on here. We sat and I explained the location as it pertained to the story. Bill, the location manager, was looking around the lot now and said he could see the advantages of filming here, lots of space and wide open for the crew. We talked about an hour and Bill was drawing out a sketch of the place and noting filming angles. The men looked at each other and said that they where happy with everything here and should go to the studio as it was getting late. I told the men to go to the car, I would be along shortly. I took Buck over to Celeste and greeted her.

"Well, your home is going to be immortalized in film for the generations." I grinned at Buck.

"Yep, but I want a walk-on, so I can be immortalized too." He grinned his walrus grin and I laughed.

"They can put you in with the bikers, I want a walk-on also." I said.

I turned to Celeste and said that we hadn't found out anything about her stalker, but to just hang in there till he comes around again, and not to worry with Buck on guard. She thanked me and said this is the most excitement she's had in a while. I turned to Buck; he said they were going back to her place in case Nelson would show up. I cautioned him again and said I'd be in touch, we shook and I went to the car.

I drove the men down the I-94 freeway to Nine Mile, the closest route to the studio, and over to Eight Mile, down Ryan Road to McNichols Road. The studio was built by local businesses to encourage Hollywood to film here, and the studio had taken over an abandoned auto parts manufacturing factory, refurbished and made to look new.

We pulled in the huge parking lot, went to the main entrance and were greeted by a rather attractive red-head at a small counter in the lobby. Scott told the woman who we were, she smiled and called someone to come and take us in. About two minutes later, a young man came, greeted us and took us to an office where the two men would set up their operations.

My cell phone rang and it was Trapper. I went out to the hallway and told him what I was up to. He said he wasn't going to ask who was playing his part, but if I knew to tell him. I said I didn't.

"I'm about five miles from Earl Daws; I may call him to warn that I'm in the area, just in case I needed him." I said.

Trapper laughed and said, "You're a paranoid P.I. and what could go wrong while filming a movie?"

Made for TV Murders

"Okay, I agree. On another note, do me a favor and check with the New York Times and see where my book was at in the rankings."

He laughed and said he'd check online, "The reviewers of your book had good things to say, the critics weren't as kind, but they never are."

"Well, as Mark Twain once said, 'The public is the only critic whose opinion is worth anything at all'. He had great book sales, and didn't care about some critic's personal opinion." I said I'd keep him informed on the movie progress and we hung up.

I wandered down the hall towards a door with a sign saying "Soundstage A". I opened the door and went in, it was the part of the original factory that must have had huge machinery to stamp and bend metal into car parts, it was a huge room. Perfect for building large sets to film on.

I was standing looking at the room when someone grabbed my arm. I had spent a good number of boring days in my office practicing drawing my Glock from its holster, and I had gotten pretty fast at it. So I did my quick draw and spun around pointing the gun at the head of a security guard. He looked stunned, letting my arm go and held his hands up.

"Not a good thing to do, man, sneak up behind a person and grab on. Could get you killed." I said as I re-holstered my Glock.

Bob Moats

He was in his late seventies by my estimate, thin, and balding by the amount of hair showing under his hat. He must be a retiree working as a guard for minimum wage. He looked like he wasn't sure what to say, so I said, "What's your name, chief?"

"Wendell Maxx." He said with a slight smile now. I knew a guy named Maxx years ago, but he said he wasn't related when I asked.

"I used to be a security guard running around a car dealership a few years ago, but I see by your patch, you don't work for them." I offered.

"I've been with this company for only a few weeks, they had an ad in the Macomb Daily for guards here; they were talking about your movie being filmed here." He said.

"My movie? How did you know it was mine?" I wondered.

"I've seen your picture in the news and they mentioned how your book was being turned into a TV show. The security company said it was being filmed here, so I applied." He was smiling now.

"Have you read my book?" I asked.

"Of course, I enjoyed it very much, you're a good writer. Another reason I wanted to work here, to meet you."

Made for TV Murders

I wasn't sure how to take that, did I have a fan or a stalker? Well, he seemed harmless enough. "Thanks Wendell, it's good to know people like my work. So how many hours do they have you working here?"

"I'm on full time while the production is going; I always wanted to see a show being filmed, so I volunteered for the extra hours." He said, still smiling.

"Well, I hope you enjoy it." I said.

Scott came through the door; he must have seen me through the window. "Jim, could you run me over to the car rental place so we can get that taken care of?"

I excused myself from Wendell and went out the door with Scott. He and I went to the limo and I drove him over to Gratiot Avenue, where there was an Avis car rental store front. I waited for him and then gave him a county map that I had in the limo, to help him get around. I opened it up and pointed out a number of places for food and drink. He thanked me.

"I won't be needing you any more for now, I'll call in the morning and we'll continue the exploring. Oh, and we'll need a motel closer to the studio, so please check on that for me." He shook my hand and got in the car he rented and drove off.

I was wondering at what speed do people from the West coast travel at. I know we are slower in the Midwest, but we enjoy life more. I got back in the limo and went up Gratiot and over to the house. As I pulled in the drive, I could see that Penny was home, her car was in the garage, and I wondered what she had in store for me tonight from her show.

*

Chapter 12

I carefully opened the front door and stuck my head in to see if there was anything going on in the living room. It was quiet so I stepped in, and I was suddenly bombarded by strange foam rubber projectiles and Nerf balls. I held my arms up to protect me, but the things just kept coming. I went to crouch behind the couch and carefully looked over and saw Penny with a couple of strange looking guns in her hands. She saw my head come up and started firing again. I yelled, "You'll run out of ammo soon. Then you're gonna get it." She yelled back, "You'll never take me alive copper." I was feeling silly lying on the floor avoiding what were harmless rubber projectiles, so I stood and attacked her. She screamed and yelled that she surrendered. I held on to her after taking her weapons away, she didn't resist very hard.

"What was that all about?" I asked still holding her in an arm lock.

"Unhand me you cad!" she yelled.

Made for TV Murders

I let her go; she stood looking at me then grabbed a couple of large Nerf balls off the snack counter and threw them at me. I just stood there and took the abuse. She laughed and latched on to me with a big, wet kiss, now that was better. She broke free and started to pick up the ammo as she spoke.

"I had a rep from a toy company on the show today and he brought samples with him to give out. I grabbed a few and decided to protect my fort. Did I even wound you?" she smiled and threw another Nerf.

"Yes, but only my pride." I picked up the ball and threw it back. Willy was going nuts all during this and ran off with a big Nerf ball in his tiny jaws. The ball was almost as big as he was.

"So Sweetie, how was your day. I see you took the limo, big deals being made." she smiled.

I told her everything that went on, even about the security guard attacking me. She listened as she put all the toys back in the big box she had brought from her studio, I presumed.

"Sounds to me like you were their bitch." She smiled at me.

"What?"

"Well, sounds like they treated you like a servant, drive us here, take us there, find a new motel. Don't these people have personal assistants to handle their needs?"

"Okay, I may have been following their lead, but I didn't feel cheap." I smiled back.

"Sweetie, you don't come cheap, just tell them to get their own needs. You are the author, screenwriter and a producer, not a gofer." She went into the kitchen, I followed. I loved it when she was so forceful.

I took out my cell phone and called Harry the older, he came on, "Harry, Jim Richards here. Will you get hold of Scott and talk to him about his needs, like another motel closer to the studio; you have a telephone book in your room, use it. And tell Scott if he wants to go exploring tomorrow to give me a call. Talk later." I hung up before he could say anything. I looked to Penny, "I just became a West Coast Hollywood type."

"Oh, a tough guy now, I like."

I grabbed her by the wrist and pulled her towards the bedroom, "I'll show you how tough I can be." She laughed and followed.

About an hour later we were on the couch again flipping through the channels, nothing on. I asked if she made a TiVo of her show, she said I must really be bored with what's on. She went and turned it on and brought the remote up to start her show. We sat and watched for about a half hour when my cell rang.

"Good, a break in the boredom." I said, she smacked my arm.

It was Buck, "Hello, boss, what's up?"

"Well, we got a visit by Steve, but didn't see him, he left a note on Celeste's door saying she was a whore for letting some man stay with her and if I didn't leave, she could get killed." I could tell Buck was enjoying the moment.

"Did you call John Handley, Trapper's friend in the Warren PD?" I asked.

"Yep, he came by and looked at the note, took it in to see if they can get any prints off it, it was a murder threat, so he said they could get involved. I told him to call when they have some info."

"It sounds like Steve's watching the house, this could be serious, be careful. You need someone to watch your back, I can call Becker?"

"Well, let's see what happens first, maybe Barry would be needed later. I'll keep you on top of it." He said and we finished.

"Bad guys circling the homestead?" Penny asked.

"Yep, nothing real serious yet, but it could get worse. I'll let Trapper know about this, unless his cop friend called him already." I grinned and we went back to watching Penny's show.

After the show ended I commented on the toys I used to have when I was a kid, all metal and harmful to our health, but I made it through the years unhurt.

Penny said, "Well, this toy manufacturer was concerned for kid's safety."

"Sure and avoiding expensive lawsuits." I smiled. "I'm going to call trapper." I pulled out my cell phone and dialed.

"So who's playing me?" He asked as soon as he came on.

I made an obscene comment and continued, "No, just wanted to fill you in on our mystery man, he left a nasty note on Celeste's door, threatened death. Your buddy, Handley has the note. Hopefully they get prints and an ID."

"I'll give John a call later to see what he came up with, not in an official capacity, just morbid curiosity. So how's the movie going?"

"Two Hollywood types flew in yesterday to start the ball rolling; I have to drive them around again, scouting out locations tomorrow."

"Well, keep me informed. Later." He hung up and I looked to Penny, she smiled and then said she was going to bed, to sleep.

"Go to bed, baby. I'm going to sit here a while and relax."

"Hell, you're going to put on Cinemax and see what skin flicks are on. I know you, then you'll come in and try to wake me, but I won't budge. Do your best." She laughed and went to the bedroom.

I sat there and thought about the last week and everything that went on. I picked up the remote and turned on Cinemax, but no skin flicks, damn. I went to bed.

Next morning my cell phone rang around 7:15 and it was Bill Urban, the location manager, "Good morning, did Harry take care of your needs?" I said before he could get on my case.

"Yes, he did well enough, now do you have anywhere else we can scout out. I have a list of scenes that need backgrounds."

"Are you at the studio or the Comfort Inn?" He said the studio. "I'll be there in an hour and we can discuss locations." He agreed and we hung up.

I dressed, kissed Penny as she was getting ready for work and left. I arrived at the studio with the limo again and was surprised to see a number of Semi trucks and a couple dozen people unloading them. There were desks and large boxes, probably full of props or whatever. I parked and went in a side door and was greeted by Wendell, the security guard.

"Good morning, Wendell, busy today." I said.

"Morning, Mr. Richards, yes they started rolling in around 5 A.M. and been busy unloading all kinds of stuff. They got one of the big rooms filled with lights and things. I really enjoy this." Wendell replied looking like a kid at a circus.

"Is Mr. Bailey around?"

"Yep, he's directing all the people moving things. He told me he is in charge of getting the studio up and running, so I answer to him."

I laughed and said, "He does seem to like running things, don't let him get to you."

"Nope, I was told by my bosses what to do and I do it." He grinned.

"Good for you. Do you know where Mr. Urban is?"

"I sure do, follow me." He said and went into the hall way to the offices and we found the door to Urban's new digs. I thanked Wendell and went in.

"Jim, good to see you. How are you this fine and bright morning?" He asked, seeming a bit more relaxed than he sounded on the phone.

"I'm good; you said you had a list of scene locations you wanted to checkout?"

"Yes, have a seat and we can discuss them. Scott won't be around us anymore now that his crew has arrived, so we are free to have a little fun. I like Scott, but he is a bit of an ass sometimes."

He laughed and sat at his new desk, I sat at a chair in front and Bill pulled out a list. We talked for about an hour going through the places he wanted to see. He explained to me that some of the actual locations may not work cinematically, so we may need to fudge on the truth a bit. I was realizing that Hollywood was built on what Howard Martin, the big guy of Big Show said, It's all an illusion.

*

Chapter 13

Bill told Scott that he was going out with me and we went to the limo. I thought I probably could have brought the Crown Vic, maybe tomorrow; I didn't want to use the limo more than I had to. We drove to a number of places that were where the crimes happened and Bill was jotting notes and taking pictures with his digital camera. We spent about three hours running around, then I said we should do lunch. We went to a Burger King and sat eating.

"How long have you been doing this?" I asked Bill.

Bob Moats

"About fifteen years, I've worked for a number of studios traveling all over the globe scouting out locations for many a movie, I love it. I enjoy the travel and being part of the film making process." He was smiling as he ate.

"We hit all the places we could on your list except the TV studio where Penny worked, that's a big part of the story, and you got a good number of notes made, so are we close to finished?"

"Yeah, I'm happy with everything, but I have to call the TV station about using their facilities. I'll have to get with the director and the cinematographer when we get rolling so they can look the places over also. They need everything to be just right." He said. "You've been very helpful, thanks." He was quiet for a moment, then said, "How did you manage to get through the ordeal without loosing it. I read the book and I was amazed at the events of the crime, you and your friends did good."

"Well, I was running on adrenaline most the time and I had good people helping, both my friends and the police. The kidnapping part with Penny was probably my most horrendous time. It was chilling to loose someone that way knowing they could be murdered."

"Yes, that worked out well for you, are you and Penny still together?"

"Yep, we even got married a few months back, a Vegas wedding complete with a couple of murders." I laughed.

Made for TV Murders

"Oh, crap, yeah, the Bridezilla murders, I heard about it. Nice work." He paused, then, "Just a word between us, the studio heads are ecstatic about making this film; they plan on going all out to see it succeed. But of course they are working on a low budget, so everyone will be doing double duty on their jobs."

I was a bit overwhelmed by what he told me. "Thanks for that, I hope the film will make a difference somewhere in life."

Bill had paid for the lunch, saying I used my gas to haul them around, it was the least he could do. We left Burger King and went back to the studio. As I pulled in the drive I was surprised to see another Limo by the front entrance, Bill said it looks like the big boys are here. I parked near the other limo and we went into the building, passing Wendell who waved to us. Bill went down the main hall as I followed and a door opened ahead, then two men came out.

The first man saw Bill and called to him, "Bill, how's my man doing?" Then he looked to me, "Well, it's the esteemed Jim Richards!" He rushed to me and started shaking my hand. "Jim, I'm Howard Martin, it is a real pleasure to finally meet you in person. How are you doing?"

I smiled and said fine. The other man with Howard came up and was introduced.

"Jim this is Wayne Barrack, our director of the film, I want you two to get together and hash things out on the script. I'm excited about the progress this is taking. Listen, I have some details to attend to, you two just get acquainted and I'll talk later." He headed back down the hall to Soundstage A and disappeared through the door. I looked at Wayne, he looked at me, we both smiled at Howard's abrupt behavior.

"Howard is a bit hyperactive. I worked with him once before, so I can warn you now to expect him to come and go. I frankly think it's for the best when he does go."

"Thanks for the tip, I appreciate it. Have you read the book or the script?" I asked hoping he wasn't ready to change things around.

"I read both and congratulations on a fine piece of work. I am looking forward to getting your input on the crime. I want to bring the harsh reality to the film."

I was liking this guy. "Well, you tell me when you want to brain storm and I'll be available." I said.

"Uh, you have anything pressing right now?" He asked.

"Well, no, I'm open. Being self-employed helps, I set my own hours" I smiled.

"Yes, right, you are a P.I. now, I love that. Is it an exciting life or just routine?"

Made for TV Murders

"A little of both, I have followed spouses and been shot three times, I'll tell you all about it sometime over a beer if you indulge?" I said hoping he was a good guy.

"Hell, I'll buy the first case. Shall we find a room to talk; I have the script and your book in my briefcase."

Bill was still standing by and I apologize for ignoring him, I introduced Wayne to Bill, then Bill said he'd show us a room we can use. He smiled and said it was Wayne's new office.

"Do I get an office?" I asked with a grin.

"Yeah, down the hall, it has a sign on the door saying Men." He laughed, "No really, you will have one, a small one but it will be an office." He took us through the building and we came to a row of offices looking out on the big soundstage. It had a good view of the room through the big windows across the front, but when we entered, Wayne pulled the blinds closed and said he felt like a fish in a bowl with all the windows and the crews walking by.

Bill said he had some notes and pictures on the locations for Wayne but had to print out the pictures, he'd have them later. Wayne said no rush; he wanted to get a feel for the script first. Bill excused himself and left. Wayne motioned me to a chair and we sat.

"I want to go over a few points in the script that I need to pick your memories about the crime and what went on. I hope you're ready to be interrogated." He grinned.

"As long as I don't get waterboarded." I said, he laughed and reached for his case, opened it and took out the script and my book.

We spent the next two hours going over the lines and situations. He was listening intently as I related moments that happened to people involved, the terror and anticipation of those people. He was making notes as I spoke and he questioned. I noticed he had a good number of sticky notes throughout my book, bookmarking pages for questions I presumed.

Someone knocked at the door; I thought that was a nice change from everyone rushing about. Wayne yelled to come in and two men in suits came through the door. The lead man asked Wayne if he was the director and Wayne said he was. They shook hands, the man introduced himself as William Tillman and his companion was Ernest Braggish, executive producers on the production. William looked at me and suddenly said, "Hey, you're Jim Richards aren't you?"

"Yeah, last time I looked at my driver's license I was." He laughed.

"Well, it is good to meet you; I'd like to have a get-together with you about this project, when you have time, since you are a producer also."

"I'll make time for you, just let me know." I answered.

"I will. Wayne, we have most of the minor bit characters cast, they are here right now in a meeting to go over their parts, but we'll need your feedback on the major players." He looked at me and smiled, "I hope we get your input also."

"Sure, I don't want just anyone playing me; he has to be ruggedly handsome." I grinned.

They laughed and apologized for the interruption and said we would meet again, they went out.

"Hollywood types move fast and loose don't they?" I asked.

He smiled and said he was from Iowa, so he had to get used to the fast pace of the west coast people. I was wondering who they had for the bit actors, Wayne asked me what I was thinking, since I had a strange look on my face.

"Oh I was just thinking about who they got for the bit parts, and if they fit the bill." I said.

He smiled and stood, "Well, lets go find out, damn it, I'm the director, I need to see who I'm working with." He laughed and we went out and asked Wendell where the bit players where meeting. He pointed to a door off the side and we thanked him and went there.

Bob Moats

We went in and there was a woman leading the group, Wayne whispered to me, she was Gloria Pelzer, from Central Casting. She recognized Wayne and came over, shaking his hand. She announced to the group who Wayne was, then looked to me. Wayne introduced me and she again announced who I was.

"It's a pleasure to meet you Mr. Richards. Let me introduce you to everyone here, and what part they are playing." She proceeded to introduce each person and their part and I was happy with the selection of people, especially the women who would be murdered. I had written in the script the scenes of each woman's murder to pump up the action, so they had to have five women for the parts. She spent a few minutes time explaining the process for the new actors in the group and then called for a fifteen minute break.

A few people went outside for a smoke and I saw one woman ask Wendell a question and he pointed to the hallway, I presumed to the restroom. I turned as Gloria was asking me about the original murders and I did my best to entertain the few people who were listening. I was looking around and saw Wendell at his post, and then some men and a woman came running out of the hallway. They stopped to talk to Wendell and he got on the phone. I wondered what was going on.

A few seconds later, one of the men came rushing in and said that there was a problem in the ladies room, a woman was dead.

Chapter 14

Earl Daws grinned from ear to ear when he saw me. He gave me a bear hug that was boarding on being embarrassing.

"Damn you Jim, it figures, a murder and here you are." He laughed as he pulled me to the hall after coming in the entrance. Wendell had filled him in on the location of the restroom in question and he was heading there when he saw me.

"Murder? Have you ruled it a murder already, you just got here." I asked.

"Well, I was told she had a rope tied around her neck, unless she committed suicide, it's a murder. But after I look, I'll make the official ruling. I'm going to have my men gather everyone in the big room for questioning. How's the big guy doing." he asked, referring to Buck.

"Oh, I have him on a case of protection; a woman had a one night stand with a stalker." I said.

"Ouch, I hate those kinds of people, stalkers I mean. I know Buck will keep her safe. How's my girlfriend, Penny?" He snickered.

"She's doing great, even without you." I snickered back.

We got to the restroom and Earl let me come in with a caution. The woman was lying in a stall with a rope tied around her neck, she was definitely murdered.

"Amazing, hundreds of people wandering about and one woman has to be alone in the crapper. Fucking amazing. Hey, did Trapper tell you I thought about retiring and getting into the P.I. business?" He looked at me like he was hoping for something.

I was amazed that he shifted gears that easily, from murder to retirement. I said Trapper did tell me and I said we three could move to Vegas and start our own firm. He laughed out loud at that and said it was a definite plan.

The CSU team came and chased us out to do their thing. Earl had the entire building of people assembled in the big soundstage and just stood watching. I quietly asked him what he was doing; he said that he was watching for a look, the kind of look a killer has when he was still at the crime scene. "Ah, your black ops training again." I laughed. He said don't knock it; it has worked in the past.

Howard Martin came over and asked what was going on, how did a woman get murdered.

Made for TV Murders

"Well, sir, I don't really know that right yet, but I intend to find out, that's what the city of Detroit pays me for." Earl smiled at Martin and went silent.

Martin just stared at Earl and said, "all right officer, I'll let you do your job."

"Thank you, and it's Homicide Detective Lieutenant Earl Daws." He replied.

"Well, detective, I hope we can take care of this quickly, we have a movie to make and delays cost money."

"Sir, I shall be as quick as I can, but unless someone confesses shortly, we may be delayed for the day, until I talk to everyone here."

Martin had nothing more to say and turned to walk away. Earl smiled at me and said, "You're the hot shot P.I. so where do we start?"

I laughed, "Well, I think we need to talk to Gloria Pelzer, from Central Casting, she was in charge of the bit players and the victim was one. I also have a strange feeling and want to ask her one question."

Earl walked forward and yelled to the crowd, "Where's Gloria Pelzer?"

Gloria called that she was here and came forward. Earl asked her to follow him to an empty office. We went in and I turned to Gloria and asked her my question. "Gloria, the woman who was killed, what part was she here to play?"

Gloria looked at the clipboard she still had, ran down the list, looking to me she said, "Dee Whittenfield, murder victim number one." She suddenly had a shocked look on her face and continued, "Oh my god, the woman who was murdered in your story by strangulation." She looked flustered and I offered her a chair, she sat.

I took Earl aside and said, "Okay, coincidence? I think this is something worth looking at." He agreed and turned back to Gloria.

"Gloria, where did this woman come from and I'll need some details on her, address and phone numbers." Gloria said she would provide the info and started writing on a paper off her clip board.

Earl turned to me and said, "What? Someone loved your book so much they decided to copycat it? Now I'll have to read your book to get an idea of its progression."

"You haven't read my book? I'm hurt." I gave him a fake hurt look.

"I'm not much for reading about crimes, just solving them." He smirked.

"Yeah, but my book could teach you a few things about crime fighting."

Made for TV Murders

Gloria called to Earl and gave him the info. The woman was from the area, lived in Ferndale. "Do most of the actors live in the area?" Earl asked her. She said a lot of them were, but a number were from out of state.

I mentioned to Earl to get a list of the soon to be murdered women from the script, he looked to Gloria, said nothing until she realized the request. "Oh, yes, I'll write them all down," she replied.

I said to Gloria, "Please don't go spreading this info around, no sense in starting a panic among the other murder victims." She agreed.

"Interesting, possible murder victims from a list of already murdered victims." Earl said.

Earl took the list and told Gloria she could go. We went back out to the soundstage and Earl called a few of his detectives so he could brief them as to what to ask and what to look for, and said to pick a couple of offices to interrogate the crowd individually.

"You probably can eliminate the crew who worked together at the time of the murder, to narrow down the numbers." I offered.

Earl looked at me, "I was getting to that, I'm capable of doing my job." He looked serious, then grinned. He looked to his men and said, "What he said, now go and bring me a killer." The men went off and started to divide the people into groups and started their work.

I had to laugh to myself; Earl still had the blasé attitude and his offbeat sense of humor that I liked. He turned to me and asked if it was lunch time yet.

I said, "We could order pizza for everyone."

"Hell no, I'm not paying for it. You're the rich writer, you order. But I think a pizza is a good idea." He pulled out his cell and hit speed dial and ordered a pizza from Dominos. Amazing, he had Dominos on his speed dial. He led me to the front lobby of the building and we waited for the delivery.

"So how's life been for you since we got back from the Mob wedding?" He asked.

"Good, been working towards this film for about a week now, finished the script and locations. Now if we can get around real murder, we can get to Hollywood murder."

"I'll try to make it as painless as possible. We'll have to seal up the crime seen so everyone may have to share the men's room for a while." He smiled. One of his detectives came out and said they had narrowed it down to about ten people who were unaccounted for and they were waiting for Earl's questioning. Earl told the detective to let them sweat for a bit, he had important matters to take care of. The detective went back to the soundstage.

"What important matters?" I asked.

Made for TV Murders

"Waiting for the pizza." He laughed.

We only waited about another ten minutes, while we made small talk, and it arrived, I paid of course. Earl made a comment about me being the rich guy now, so lunch was my treat. We put the box at the reception desk, down where it wouldn't be seen and ate a couple quick pieces. Earl said, "Time to go fry some butt." We went back out to the soundstage but not before Earl grabbed another piece of pizza, I did too.

We entered the room and Earl yelled "Okay, sports fans, let's play ball!" He approached the detective who told him about the suspects and the man said the people were in the room where the bit players had their meeting, but they had them separated and had a uniform watch them so they didn't talk to each other. He led us to where they were and Earl told him to wait outside. We went in and he stood looking at all the people, doing his psychic stare down. He pointed to a man in the front and asked him to follow, then he told the others to sit tight and don't talk. He led the man to an office next to the meeting room and told the man to have a seat. I stood at the back of the room, missing the magic mirror.

"Your name is?" Earl asked.

"Perry Hall," the man said simply.

"Okay, Perry, what is it you do here?" Earl had his note pad out ready to write.

"I'm a set designer, I was sketching out the set for the real estate office scene so the construction people could start building it," he replied.

I was wondering why Bill didn't use the actual office since it was still being run by the late Joyce Harper's partners.

"You were alone during this time; no one saw you or talked to you?" Earl asked.

"I was alone yes, in the production office. No one was around."

"Did you know the woman who was murdered?" He looked at a sheet of paper he was given before coming into the room. "Her name was Helen Carter, ring a bell?"

"No, don't know her. Really."

"Have you read the Classmate Murders book?" Earl asked.

"No, I just read the script."

"Okay, Perry you can go for now, but be ready to answer any more questions I may have, go." Earl motioned to the door and Perry left. Earl called in the next suspect and went through the same line of questioning throwing in a few new ones as the moment struck him.

He finished with all ten people and sat back in his chair. "I don't get much of a vibe off any of them; maybe I need another piece of pizza to clear my mind." He smiled and we went back to the lobby.

*

Chapter 15

As we got to the pizza box Earl cursed, "Someone hit the pizza box; I got a new crime scene!" I looked and a couple of pieces were missing, leaving only one, I laughed.

"Take it; you need it more than I do." I said as I patted my beer belly.

"I was planning on it, I need the energy." He smiled as he took a bite from the piece.

"Well, I don't see anything more I can do until CSU finishes their investigation, hopefully the murderer was careless. I hate dragged out cases."

"So I can tell Martin his people can go back to work?" I asked.

"Yeah, but if anyone disappears from work, let me know." He replied. "Thanks for the pizza, next time we order Chinese."

We walked back to the soundstage and he yelled to his men to gather and told them to head back. They left and he saluted me and left.

Martin came up and asked what was going on. I told him to start production again, the crime was still being investigated, but he was good to go. He smiled and yelled for Scott Bailey to get it moving again. Everyone clamored to get back to their jobs and Martin asked Scott if they had a medical room set up for injuries, Scott said the field nurse was coming in today and he'd have it ready for her. Martin said good and the two men walked away.

I stood by myself when I heard a voice behind me, "Quite a morning, Mr. Richards." I turned to see Wendell standing quietly behind me.

"Yes, Wendell, it has been. I don't want to have to live these murders over again in real life, the first time was enough. Did they talk to you too?"

"Yes they did, one of the detectives asked me a number of questions and then finished with me." He smiled. "I hope I don't get yelled at by my bosses for letting this happen while I was on watch." His smile faded.

"There wasn't much you could have done Wendell. If they give you a hassle I would be more than happy to tell them were to go for you."

"Oh, I think I can handle it, I don't want to stir up trouble." He smiled again and went back to his post at the door.

I looked at my watch and it was going on 5:30, I saw Wayne and went to him. "Is there anything further you need me for today?" I asked.

He smiled and said he was going to go over plans for the production with the cinematographer when he came in, then he was going to collapse for the night, long trip out and all. I said I'd be back in the morning, he said he'd watch for me.

I went out to the limo and drove home slowly thinking about all the occurrences of the day and meeting Earl again, it was like old times. I thought about how much fun it could be to have Earl and Trapper working together in our own firm. I was on auto pilot again and found myself in the drive. I parked and covered the limo and looked to the Crown Vic and decided to take it tomorrow. I went up to the door and into the living room, and found Penny sitting with a rather attractive woman, I suddenly recognized her, the movie actress Tia Brinkman. Penny jumped up and greeted me, giving me a big hug and a kiss, then took me to the couch where Brinkman was lounging.

"Jim, I'm sure you know who this is?" Penny was glowing.

"Yes, Miss Brinkman, it's a pleasure to meet you." I was almost stuttering at being in the room with this famous academy award nominated actress.

She jumped up and gave me a bear hug and said, "I would kiss you like Penny does, but I didn't ask for permission."

I must have looked confused, Penny said that Tia was the actress who was playing her in the movie. I was a bit stunned by that announcement and asked how she got here, there was no car in the drive.

"Tia was on my show today talking about the movie, it was a last minute scheduling by my producer to promote the movie and that it's being made here in Detroit. I invited Tia to stay with us to get to know my quirks and we drove together."

Tia smiled and said, "I want to study Penny to get her personality into my character, you don't mind do you?"

"Oh, god no, but I don't know if I can take all this beauty under one roof." I smiled.

"You're right Penny, he is charming." Tia gave a smirk like Penny would, it was a bit unnerving.

"Well, have you two had dinner yet?" I asked and they said no, "Well, I'll treat to a nice meal at a fancy restaurant if you'd like."

Made for TV Murders

Penny said, "That means Burger King." They both laughed the same, now I was about freaking out.

"I'd love a good home cooked meal if it's not too much trouble, I eat out so often it's getting tiring." Tia asked.

Penny said she could whip up a lasagna and salad if that was good, Tia said that sounded great and wanted to help. Penny told me to relax and they went off to the kitchen. Willy was standing by my feet and I picked him up and whispered in his ear, "I think we're in trouble."

We had dinner at the dining room table, nothing fancy; Tia wanted it to be like we usually do it so she could get a feel for Penny.

"Well, we usually just camp out on the couch with beer and chips watching lousy TV." I laughed. "You'll have to camp with us if you want to get the real Penny down." Penny whacked my arm and then Tia whacked my other. "Damn, am I going to get double barrels now from both of you?"

"Penny filled me in on ways to bug you, so be prepared." Tia grinned.

I just sat and said nothing in my defense, wouldn't do any good.

"Okay on a somber note, I have to tell you about a new development that happened today." I said solemnly. "There was a murder at the studio today; a woman was strangled in the ladies room." I paused for effect and looked to Penny. "She was the actress who was going to play Dee." Penny was shocked and knew who I was talking about, and the back-story of her death, but she explained it to Tia.

"Oh my God, what happened?" Tia asked.

"Well, the police came and have nothing yet, but they are investigating. The woman was in the restroom and someone slipped in and strangled her, that's all I can tell you."

Penny said, "Murder just follows you around doesn't it, I always say that don't I?"

I had to smile at that even if it was a serious matter. "Yes, she always says that every time there's a murder and we're around." I said to Tia.

"Have they stopped the production?" Tia asked.

"No, the police said they could go on." I looked at Penny, "The lead detective was Earl Daws."

"Earl! How is he doing, not corrupted by his affiliation with the mob is he?" Penny asked.

"Nope, he's just as crazy as he was when we stormed New York City." I explained to Tia what we were talking about.

"Wow, you two do lead exciting lives, don't you?" She smiled.

"Well, unfortunately it usually involves someone loosing their life, that's not a good thing." They agreed.

"Tell me Tia, did you get cast through auditions or did Howard just pick you?" I asked, changing the subject.

"Yes, Howard called me earlier in the week and asked if I would be interested, and I'll admit I had read your book. I love crime stories, especially true crime ones. I enjoyed your book and told Howard that if I didn't get the part I would find him and ... Well, I won't say what part of him I would cut off, but you get the idea." She laughed like Penny, I thought this actress was a quick study of people, or she was Penny's lost twin.

"Howard kept telling me I would be included in the decisions to select the actors but I guess he has his own ideas on who he wants." I said looking a bit disturbed.

"Jim, take Howard as he is, he does things on his own, but trust him, he makes good decisions. You'll be happy." She smiled and stood to gather the dishes.

"You don't have to do that." Penny insisted.

"This is something you do, so I have to play the part." She replied.

Penny just grinned and said, "I usually force Jim to do the dishes, he grumbles, but I say I won't give him any sex if he doesn't."

"Do I get to practice having sex with him?" Tia asked Penny.

I sat squirming as Penny said go for it.

*

Chapter 16

We spent the evening crashed on the couch with beer and chips and talking; Tia was telling gossip about actors she worked with. She talked about different movies she was in and what it's like to be an actress, Penny was listening to her intently, I was worried. Penny was asking a lot of questions about how she got into films and Tia was more than eager to share some of her stories with Penny. Then Tia turned it around and asked us about our adventures with tracking down killers. Penny went into great detail about what we had gone through and Tia listened intently also.

Around midnight we started wearing down and toddled off to our bedrooms, Penny pointing to the guest room for Tia and said that she better not find Tia in our bed. Tia laughed out loud and went into the guest room.

Made for TV Murders

I laid in bed thinking about the day. Penny turned to me and whispered, "You better not be thinking about Tia." She turned back and was quiet; I thought she went to sleep. I laughed and she mumbled, "I mean it."

It was Saturday morning, so Penny didn't have to work. Penny and Tia were busy making themselves look beautiful and they said Tia had to go to the studio to meet with Howard. I was ready to go, I had decided to use the limo again, so had it parked by the porch. They came out, Tia had Willy's purse and Willy seemed a bit confused, I ruffled his head and said to just go with it.

Tia was impressed that the car was once a Mob limo and the girls sat in the back as I chauffeured them to the studio as Penny told her the story of the limo. We pulled into the studio parking lot; Howard and Wayne were standing out front talking. Howard saw Tia getting out and ran to her.

"Tia, doll! How are you, glad you could make it!" He was elated, and then he saw Penny. "My, my. Two gorgeous stars of TV and movies, this is a day." He took them up to the front doors as I stood by the car feeling left out.

Wayne laughed and said, "Howard has a narrow line of sight, especially when it comes to women, don't take it personal. He sets his priorities and sticks to them. How are you this morning?"

"I'm good, you?"

"Great, we have a number of sets built and dressed, these guys are amazing. We'll be shooting minor scenes today, with the bit people and then this afternoon, Howard has a few major actors coming in to audition for us. Tia is the only one Howard wanted in her part."

"Well, he made a good choice; Penny likes her so we're good to go."

We went in the building and out to the soundstage. They had it partitioned off and I saw where they had my old bedroom set up, I had to laugh. It looked good and messy just like my real bedroom was.

"Any word on who would play me?" I asked.

"None yet, we have three men coming in, no one real famous, sorry, but most of the leading men aren't built like you or as old, no offense."

"None taken, I am unique."

Howard called to Wayne and he excused himself and went to meet Tia and Penny. Wendell snuck up behind me again; I was going to have to keep an eye on him.

"Good morning Mr. Richards. I see you brought your lovely wife and Miss Brinkman."

"Yep, I was overwhelmed with beauty this morning." I smiled. "Any repercussions about yesterday from your bosses?"

Made for TV Murders

"Nope, they asked me about it and I told them and they said to be more watchful, which I will." Wendell smiled. "But they did send out a few more guards to watch the building and the people, so you'll see more of us around."

"Great, that makes me feel better." Wayne called me and I excused myself from Wendell and went to him.

"Jim, we're going to be filming the murder of Dee Wittenfield and the kennel murder of Marge Holden. We can't do Joyce Harper's murder yet till we cast your part and Trapper. So if you could stand by, I may want to confer with you about that scene later." He smiled and went to a person setting up the camera equipment, I presumed the cinematographer.

I saw that they had replaced the murdered actress with a new girl and they were talking to her as the stage workers were getting the shower scene set up. I looked over to my right and there was a set made up to look like a kennel for Marge's murder.

Everyone was set up and ready to go when I heard a familiar voice behind me. It was Trapper along with Barry Becker in uniform.

"Hey, when did you two get here?"

"About an hour ago, Wayne called me and asked if I could come in to talk about a number of scenes I was involved in to give my take. Its odd seeing this all again. And I hear you had a real murder yesterday, tell me about it after we finish here." Wayne yelled for Trapper and he went to explain to Wayne the positioning and events of the actual shower killing. I asked Becker how he was doing, he said good and was excited about being here. He whispered that the director had asked him if he wanted to play his own part since it was so small, he jumped at the chance. I smiled at Becker's wide-eyed innocence.

Wayne called for a run through and they walked through the steps of the scene and did this a couple of times, then Wayne called for a take.

The assistant director called for quiet on the set and they ran the parts of the killing in the shower. It was so real looking, I squirmed a bit thinking about my Dee dying like that. They reset for some close ups of the killer sneaking in the window and escaping. Then they had the background police actors busting down the door to get to her. The scene ended and Wayne was happy as he looked through his little TV that showed the way it was being filmed.

"Great people, it's in the can. Let's set up for the kennel murder." He moved over to the kennel set as the grips got everything ready for the shot. Wayne called for the actress playing Marge Holden and we stood around waiting. Wayne called again and then yelled for Gloria. Gloria came running and said the actress was here a few minutes ago. Trapper came back to me and smiled from ear to ear, he was in his glory for his part helping with the scene.

113

Made for TV Murders

Voices came from behind the kennel set calling for help and people went running. Behind the fake wall of the kennel lay the body of the actress, her head bleeding badly. Trapper moved to the front and yelled for everyone to get back, flashing his badge, he checked her and said she was dead. I got on my phone speed dial and called Earl, he wasn't going to like this.

"Trapper, you old warthog, you just had to stick your nose in didn't you?" Earl yelled to Trapper as he came in, followed by his men again. Earl gave Trapper a bear hug, Earl liked doing that. Trapper took Earl to the crime scene and Earl called to his men to do it again, same routine. The detectives called for people to follow them.

Howard came over and was worried that his people were at risk. Trapper spoke this time, "Well, it seems the only people who are being murdered are the women who are playing the murdered women." Earl said he'd have some of his men protecting the rest if they could tell him who they were. Howard said he'd have Gloria get with him and arrange the protection. Howard asked if Earl could assign a cop to Tia Brinkman pointing her out, Earl looked over and I could see his eyes glow.

He walked past Howard and went straight to Tia and introduced himself. Earl called to a uniform standing by the door and ordered him to guard Miss Brinkman with his life. He said he'd like to talk more to her later and came back to us.

"Your testosterone is showing." I laughed.

"Damn, do you see who that is? Tia Brinkman, my dream girl. Tidal Basin, View from the Top, Killing floor, A Little Romance... I've seen all her movies at least twice."

"Yeah, and she slept in my home last night." I said, then Earl's head snapped around. He asked if she was staying with Penny and me. I told him she was playing Penny, so she was staying with us for a few days to study Penny.

"Jim, old buddy, invite me over for a visit, please." He was just about begging.

"Damn, big tough black ops boy turns to putty." I laughed and Trapper snorted.

"Come on Jim, please, just one evening."

"I'll see what Penny says, but I see no problem." I answered.

Trapper asked, "What about me?" I said I'd invite everyone over and we would make it a party.

*

Chapter 17

The questions were asked, everyone was interrogated again, nothing was solved, and Earl was getting a bit pissed off. Trapper was enjoying watching his friend have a minor melt down with Tia around. She was now following Earl asking questions about his police work. I was wondering if there was a romance in the future, since Earl had put his men to work now and spent more time talking to Tia. Admittedly, Earl was a handsome man, I could see why Tia would like him, a cop and good looking to boot. Tia had said last night that she liked crime mysteries, and Earl was a crime mystery in himself. I knew Tia was in her late fifties now, but she was like Penny, youthful and a beauty. Earl was in his late forties, maybe early fifties, so I guess the age difference didn't bother him.

Earl took time from flirting with Tia, and was expressing his concern to us over the lack of evidence, and that out of about fifty people in the studio, no one saw anything. We went into an office, Earl, Trapper and I and sat going over the events of this day. I told Earl everything I observed.

"Everyone was concentrating on the shower scene; the woman was wearing modesty cover but was mostly naked, so the men were all paying attention to her. It would have been easy for the killer to follow the vic to the back of the set and do a quick whack on the head.

116

But this doesn't follow the original pattern, Marge was the third woman killed, Joyce should have been next."

Trapper offered, "Well, that scene couldn't be filmed because they didn't have the principle actors yet, so the killer took what he had. This killer is trying to mess with the production by killing the women before they get to appear in it. He's not caring whose next."

"Or she, we can't rule out that it could be a woman." Earl said.

"Could a woman have strangled the first vic?" I asked.

"Don't let some of these women hear that. I saw a few that could lift me off the ground." Trapper laughed.

"Well, we need to watch the actress portraying Joyce carefully. I'm also wondering if this killer is going to come forward with some kind of statement, like the killers in your book." Earl said.

"You read it? When did you read it?" I asked.

"Last night, I picked it up at Walden Books yesterday and read it in bed." he smiled.

"I suppose you took a speed reading course like Trapper did?" I asked.

Trapper said, "We took the class together, we had a challenge going to see who could read the fastest."

Made for TV Murders

"You guys are pathetic." I smiled.

A detective came in the room and said they were finished with the suspects and the ME had removed the body, it was blunt force to the head that killed her. He said it was the same suspect situation as yesterday, nothing jumping out about the killer. We went out and Earl told Howard he could continue with the film but to have his crew be on alert watching the women. Howard was looking really distressed and said he would. Earl said he didn't have much more to do till CSU made their report, he went over to Tia and they talked briefly, he gave her his card, and then he left.

Tia and Penny came to Trapper and I, Penny was carrying Willy now. "This is serious isn't it; I mean that the classmate killers are surfacing again. Why?"

"I wish I knew. There hasn't been any word from the killer about the murders, so we haven't any idea who may be behind it or why. Time will tell." I said.

Howard came by and told Trapper and I that they had the principle actors in for auditions, if I wanted to participate. I said I did. He took us to the front offices and into a fairly large conference room. I asked Trapper where Becker was, he said he had to go back to the station, they needed him. I said I supposed I'd have to drive Trapper back with the women; he smiled and said that was his plan. I laughed and said he was as bad as Earl.

Bob Moats

In the room there were about ten people along with Wayne, Howard and Gloria, who were standing at the front of the room. Wayne spoke first.

"Ladies and gentlemen, we will be running everyone through the paces that I'm sure you are used to by now, thank you for all coming out, you are all respected in your craft and we will make this as quick and painless as possible." Wayne introduced Tia, standing with us at the back of the room along with Penny, who Tia was portraying, then he introduced me as the author of the book and the real Jim Richards of the movie. He gave a nod to Trapper and then asked for the first person to follow him to a room where they would do the auditions.

My little group went to the next office and sat back watching each person go through the motions of reading and acting. Trapper was whispering to me that none of these men had his charm or bravado. The men who were going for my part were good, I liked two of them, plus they were both halfway known character actors that I had seen in films and TV, so it was good. After they had ran through all the actors, Wayne and Gloria came over and asked for our opinion, I gave him mine and Trapper said he could do his own acting, Wayne laughed and said no. Wayne said to me that he liked Leo Brooks for my part, he presently was an actor on a cable police show, I agreed. Wayne announced to Trapper his choice to play him and Trapper had to agree, saying he was all right.

Made for TV Murders

"Wayne, are the actors who will be playing Buck coming in?" I asked.

Gloria spoke now. "Actually we already cast him and he will be in tomorrow, his name is Vince Morris and he is as close to Buck as we could get. Big, macho and a real biker off camera. He usually plays the bad guy on TV and movies, and he was anxious to be in this part. He's also a former stand-in and stunt double for Hulk Hogan in movies featuring Hogan."

I thought that would at least please Buck, as this guy was close to Hulk Hogan. I was wondering what Buck was up to now and thought about calling him when we were done here. I asked Gloria about the motorcycle club that would be needed later; she said she was going to locate them soon. I gave her the phone number from my Palm TX for Luther and told her these were the actual people from the original incident; she thanked me and said she would call him.

Someone came in and said that they had a replacement for the part of Marge and were ready to film. Wayne went out after telling everyone of his decisions and the actors all vacated the room leaving the selected actors to confer with Gloria. Wayne went out and we tagged along to watch. The filming of the kennel killing went well and Wayne was pleased. He called everyone together and said in respect for the murdered victims, he was calling off work for the rest of the day, till tomorrow, when the principle actors would be in to film. He thanked everyone and came over to us.

"I'll need you and Trapper in tomorrow morning if you can, we'll start really getting into the script now and I'd like both your input. I want this to be as close to the actual incident as possible. So, see you guys in the morning?" We agreed and he went off. I looked at Trapper, then Penny and Tia, and said I guess we can go. I mentioned that Trapper was coming with us, and the cop watching Tia said he'd be back in the morning also.

We went to the side exit; Wendell said good-night to us as we went through the door, out to the parking lot. Unfortunately we were overrun by a gaggle of news reporters all standing around waiting for a sound byte. I was a bit shocked to see them, and they swarmed around us. I was in the lead followed by Penny and Tia, then Trapper guarding from the rear. Right away the questions were flying and I was trying to deflect their intrusions. I really didn't like news people; they weren't my favorite people, just below politicians and lawyers. They were getting in my face and I was starting to get annoyed. They recognized Tia and started to bother her. Trapper was pushing back the vultures from her and then flashed his badge and yelled the next man who touches Tia would be arrested.

I heard one man yell that this sounded like a publicity stunt for the movie. I spun around and got in his face. "Listen asswipe, two women had their lives snuffed out and this is no publicity stunt, but you assholes will make it a big newsbreak and give all the wrong facts, doesn't matter to you, because you don't care for the truth anyways, now get the fuck away from us." I was hot.

I opened the door to the limo and let the women and Trapper get in, closed the door and gave the finger to the cameras as the reporters were still throwing out questions. One reporter yelled out, asking who I was. I smiled as I went to the driver's door and said, I'm just the chauffeur. I got in and sped out of the lot.

*

Chapter 18

After I got everyone safely home, dropping Trapper off at his precinct, I called Buck to see how he was doing. He came on after two rings and gave me his big happy greeting.

"Anything new on the stalker front?" I asked.

"Nope, the guy is laying low. Handley came back today to say they couldn't find any prints on the letter other than Celeste's and mine. The guy was being cautious and probably wore gloves knowing we would call the cops. He's playing us."

"Well, keep an eye on her, and let me know if anything develops." I asked.

Buck hung up and turned to Celeste, "I know we haven't talked a lot about this guy, but I think we should put our heads together and see what we can come up with." Buck took Celeste to her dining table and they sat. "Okay, talk to me about the night you two met?"

"Well, I went with two of my friends from work out to a bar off Harper and the freeway by Fifteen Mile Road. We were just relaxing and enjoying the music when this guy came up and asked me to dance. I thought for a minute, then said yes. Well, he was a good dancer and we were out dancing for a while. The music stopped for a break and I went to sit, he followed and asked if he could buy me and my friends a drink. Free drink, sure. We talked about nothing much really, just the economy and celebrities. I asked him about himself and he was kind of vague, but said he worked for a loan company in Sterling Heights. He said he lived there also; he had an apartment by himself. That was about all he said about himself, he kept changing the subject back to me. Well, we had a good number of drinks and my two friends said they were going to leave, I didn't want to go and Steve said he'd drive me home. My friends were anxious to go and they just left us alone. I have to wonder about my friends. They left and we dance some more, then left."

She paused and Buck asked if she wanted a glass of water or pop, Celeste went to get two cans of Sprite that Buck bought earlier and gave him a can. "You can guess what happened after we got here, he stayed the night, it was early Sunday when we got back here, so when we woke he said he had to go to take his mother to church. He left by 7 A.M. and he got my number before he left. I asked for his and he said he just had his cell phone but the minutes were out, he had to re-fill them before he could use it. I should have known when he wouldn't give me his number. I'm not real stupid."

"I'm sure you're not, but it wasn't the best thing to bring a stranger home. Now tell me anything about the guy you can remember, describe him, hair, eyes, any tattoos on him that you remember?" Buck asked.

"Yes, he did have a tattoo, on his left arm just above his elbow. It was a strange design, I asked him about it and he said it was a... How did he say it... a gang tat, I think was what he said."

Buck's ears perked up to that, "What did it look like?"

"I can't really describe it, here, I'll draw it out." She took a pad of paper and pencil from her kitchen counter behind her, and started to draw the symbol. She finished and handed it to Buck. He took one look and smiled.

"I have to make a few phone calls, but I think we may be able to track this guy down now." He took out his cell phone and called Luther.

Penny and Tia were in the kitchen chattering way so Willy and I stayed out in the living room watching television. It suddenly got quiet out there and the curiosity got the better of me. I snuck to the kitchen and heard voices from the porch. I went to the edge of the door and listened, then peeked around the corner, Tia was standing watching Penny spin around the stripper pole. I watched for a couple of seconds then moved over and gave Penny applause. That startled both women and Penny came to a screeching halt. She gave me a grin and came over to give me a kiss. She turned to Tia and said I was her best audience. Tia laughed and asked if she could try the pole, Penny said go for it. She latched on and did a whole lot of moves that had Penny just standing with her mouth open.

Tia came off the pole and laughed, "Sorry, I couldn't resist, I played a stripper in one of my movies, Night Heat, and I had worked hours with a professional to get the moves right."

"Well, you succeeded in learning. Now you'll have to teach me a couple of things I saw you do." Penny said and went to the pole.

I was watching them discuss the finer points of pole dancing when I heard the door bell. I grumbled about timing and went to answer. I peeked through the small window at the top of the door and yelled out, "No one home!" Earl's voice yelled back, "I have a warrant." I yelled back, "I don't care, no one home."

"Come on, Jim. Let me in." He sounded so pitiful, I opened the door and asked what he wanted, it was late and he wasn't invited. He grinned and said he wanted to discuss the case with me, besides the killer sent a message. My heart took an extra beat and I let him in.

"This better not be a lie to get inside." I threatened.

"Nope, totally legit, the email came around four o'clock and it was addressed to me. Had me wondering how he knew where to send it, but it's not hard to find out." He pulled out a paper from his jacket pocket and handed it to me. I was just going to read from the paper when Penny and Tia came into the room. Tia immediately went to Earl and got all gushy, it reminded me of Deacon and Lynn when they first met. I went to Penny and said to watch them carefully. I read the note.

"Detective Daws, you have done an admirable job of questioning all the wrong people in regards to the actress murders. You won't find much from them as I have covered my tracks well. Why, you ask, am I killing these women, it is revenge. Revenge for what, you will have to figure that out. Oh, and make sure Jim Richards is involved in this case, I want to see him squirm when I take his most precious possession from him as he took from me." I was puzzled at that statement. "I'm sure you will be extra careful in protecting the rest of the cheerleaders, but I will get to them, especially the last cheerleader. She will be my final score to make. Good luck, you will need it. Disrespectfully yours, the Avenger." I saw the P.S. at the bottom and it read, "Be sure to have the delightful Detective Trapper help with the case, I want to be sure he suffers most of all." That had me worried.

I looked to Earl who was totally entranced by Tia, who was twisting him around her finger. "Earl, do you have the complete headers for this email?" I asked. He took his attentions from Tia and said, "it came from, wait for it... Pompo Deli."

"Crap, Stacy is going to have a coronary." I said.

"Who?" Earl asked.

"I thought you read my book. Stacy, the waitress at Pompo Deli."

"Ah, yes, I remember now. We'll have to call Trapper in on this."

"Well, the threat includes him. May as well."

Penny looked at me, "What are you two babbling about?"

I handed her the note and said it came from the killer. She read it and handed it back, "I'm not really liking this, can we go out to Vegas till Earl solves it."

"Hey, the note specifically says I am involved." I handed the note to Earl and Tia asked if she could see it.

"Okay, he, or possibly she, says that it's for revenge, and he mentions the cheerleaders, so it has something to do with the original crime or a copycat from the book. He knows of the movie, and this is his way of committing his revenge, but why innocent actresses, they had nothing to do with the original crime. They're just playing the parts. He also says he wants the last cheerleader to die most of all, but which cheerleader, Tia who is playing her or Penny who was her. He mentions taking my most precious possession from me, which would be Penny, but I don't consider her a possession." I looked at her and she gave me a half-assed smile, probably not happy with being threatened. "And what did I take from him, and who the hell is him. He wants Trapper to suffer the most, why? Trapper was the cop on the original case, but he really didn't do much, no offence to his abilities, but Deacon, Buck and I did most the leg work and we stopped the killers."

There was a knock at the door, Earl said, "That's probably Trapper, I called him on my way here."

I grimaced and said, "Oh, good, now we can party."

*

Chapter 19

We filled Trapper in on what had transpired and he stood thinking. "It sounds like Jim said, someone from the original case or a copycat. He must have read the book and is living out the original murders this way, the only way he can get his jollies off." He apologized to the woman, then said, "The only thing I really did was shoot Alice Stone, so is she the connection to my threat?"

"Maybe we should check on her husband, he might want you dead for shooting her?" I said to Trapper.

"That's a thought; I'll take Becker there tomorrow to check on him. How's protection going to go now for the film?" Trapper asked.

I told everyone to sit, Earl and Trapper escorted Tia to the couch, they sat, Tia was sitting between Earl and Trapper, I thought both their heads would explode.

Earl said, "I can assign a few men to the production, but I'm spreading them thin. The studio should bring in more of their security to watch the women. I'll talk to Howard Martin and arrange it with him."

I asked if anyone wanted something to drink, then took the drink orders. I went into the kitchen, then I saw Tia come in.

"Jim, tell me about Earl and Trapper." She asked.

"Well, you read in my book about Trapper, that was basically him, Earl is another matter. He is a former Federal agent, CIA and NSA, got tired of the governmental rat race and became a cop. He's mysterious and a bit goofy. I could tell you more but we don't have the time, maybe later if you really are curious." I smiled.

She laughed and helped take the drinks out. Penny came into the kitchen before I left and asked if Tia and I were fooling around.

"No, we weren't. She was asking me about Earl and Trapper, I fear for their lives." I smiled and kissed her on the nose. We took the rest of the drinks out to the living room and relaxed.

My cell phone rang, I saw from the ID that it was Buck, I excused myself and went to the porch and sat at my desk in the corner.

"Hey partner, what's up?"

"Well, I got a lead on our stalker. I had a talk with Celeste, which I should have done earlier, and she gave me some info on a tattoo he wore. It was a biker gang tat and I called Luther for any info on it. He said he'd look into it and call me back. What's happening on the movie?"

I told him about the latest murder and the email we got today and he whistled. "You going back to Pompo to shake up Stacy again." Buck laughed.

"I hate to do it, but it needs to be done. She's going to quit her job if she finds out her café is a gathering place for murderers. If you weren't busy with Celeste, I'd have you watch Penny and Tia."

Buck laughed and said, "Why don't you see if Angelo has a few Mob connections in Detroit and get some gorillas to help watch the women."

"Actually that's not such a bad idea, but I don't think I'll involve the Mob right now. Keep me informed on your progress and talk later."

He said he would and we finished. I looked down and Willy was sitting at my feet watching me. I figured he hadn't been fed so we went to the kitchen and I opened a can of dog food for him, he was wolfing it down as I went back to the living room. I filled Trapper in on what Buck had said.

"I'll probably get a call from Handley about it tomorrow, unless Buck goes off on his own investigation. I wouldn't put it past him." Trapper grinned.

"Buck can handle himself. Plus, he has Luther and the rest of his friends to help now." I replied.

We sat and talked about life and the world in general and then around eleven o'clock, I announced it was time for our guests to vacate the premises. Earl and Trapper grumbled about it, but gave their good-nights and got ready to leave, but not before Tia gave each one a kiss on the cheek and thanked them for helping to keep her safe. Trapper said he'd track down Alice Stone's husband tomorrow and let me know what he finds. They went off and Penny took Tia back out to the stripper pole, she wanted more lessons. I plopped down on the couch with my beer and Willy cuddled up to me, then I turned on Cinemax, they finally had a skin flick on, so I was happy.

Made for TV Murders

The next morning, Sunday, we got ready to go to the studio. I called Howard and he said that he believed in people's right to go to church, so they wouldn't be starting until later in the day. I told him about the email Earl had and that Earl would be in touch with him about security. Howard said he had talked to the studio's security guard company and was increasing protection. Besides his insurance company wasn't happy about the mess, so they insisted he step up the guards.

I took the women out to the Crown Vic this time and I drove them to a local Big Boys and treated them to breakfast. A number of people in the restaurant recognized Tia and had to ask for autographs. We sat and ate, talking about the murders and Tia was commenting on Penny's life with me. Penny was complimentary about me and her life with me. I just sat, ate my breakfast and smuggled bits of food to Willy, who was hiding in his purse next to me.

We finished our breakfast and went back out to the Crown Vic; Tia got in back and commented on how she had a number of flings in the back of a car just like mine. I asked if she'd like me to call Trapper or Earl and she laughed out loud and said no thank you. We got to the studio around noon and there were a number of people getting ready for the shoot today. I saw the new actors playing the principle roles were getting made-up and costumed. I went to the man who was playing my part and he jumped up to greet me.

"Mr. Richards, it's an honor to meet you and portray you too." He smiled. I didn't feel like I was looking into a mirror, but I thought the resemblance was there in spirit.

"Thanks, but please call me Jim, after all you are me." I smiled. "Do you have your lines committed to memory already?" I asked.

"I've always been good at remembering lines. It really helps in this business to be prepared and ready to go. Directors like that."

"Have you ever worked with Wayne before?" I wondered.

"I had a bit part in one of his films, so small the assistant director took care of my scenes. So I just watched him work, he is good."

That made me feel better. "What are they setting up to film today?" I asked.

"Well, the scenes of you in your room, finding the first email from Dee, and then the scenes from the Realty office with Joyce Harper."

"Were is the actress who is playing her?"

"Look for an older woman flanked by two huge security guards; it will most likely be her." He laughed. I thought that he had a good sense of humor, like me, I approved. I thanked him and wandered till I ran into Trapper and Becker talking to Tia and Penny. Trapper has good radar.

"Good morning to Clinton Township's finest police." I said as I approached and I acknowledged Barry Becker.

Trapper grinned and said, "We've been here since eight o'clock, I didn't know they were sticklers about Sunday mornings. But we did scout out the premises to see if a killer could be hiding anywhere."

Wayne came flying in the side door and called out to see if everyone was ready to get back on schedule. Scott Bailey came over to him and they were talking quietly then Scott went off to the front offices. Wayne saw us and came over.

"No problems I hope." I asked him.

"No, Scott was just telling me about the extra security that was around the building. This place is going to be run like an Army post." He laughed as Gloria came up and said the actors were ready to go.

"Okay, let's rock and roll." He said and went off to where they were going to film my bedroom scenes. Wayne called me over and asked me about that night, when I got the first email from Dee. We talked a bit, then he lined up everyone and did a run through on the scene. He was pleased and called for a take, and for the next hour they worked on the fine details of my night. Wayne was happy with the scenes and called for the realty office scene with Joyce and Jim. It sounded strange to be referred to like I wasn't there.

They started the scene from where Joyce and I came into the office and ran through it a few times, then committed it to film. The police extras were called in for when Trapper enters the building. My Trapper was excited to watch his counterpart act out the incident. Becker was trying not to grin as he took his part in the scene.

"Fine, Becker gets to be in the movie, I think I should have played myself." Trapper lamented.

"Barry's role is tiny, give the kid his moment." I said.

The scene went well as Becker let the fake Jim out the door, and then they set up for the poisoning scene. I wasn't there back when it actually happened, so Trapper gave his input to Wayne. I noticed that the props had been set out and then they started to run it through. I don't know why, but my tingle went off. I walked forward and went to the actress who was going to drink from the cup of poisoned coffee and stopped her. I asked if I could see the cup and she handed it to me. I held it up and took a sniff then called Trapper. He came over and I held out the cup for him to smell.

He looked to me and said, "Unless they added Almonds to this brew, we got cyanide."

*

Chapter 20

Earl carefully handed the coffee cup to the CSU officer and turned to me. "How'd you know it was poisoned?"

"I didn't, but it just stood to reason, each woman was being murdered by the book, so when I saw the actress getting ready to sip from the cup, it just didn't feel right. So I checked." I replied.

"Good you did, saved one woman from a painful death. I've seen cyanide poisonings before, not pleasant." He said.

"Are you sure you didn't poison a few cups of coffee yourself?" I grinned. He just gave me a blank look and said, "Who me?"

Wayne was standing by us and Earl asked him who the prop person was, Wayne turned and yelled for someone named Jane. A young woman of about thirty, tall, thin, long blond hair moved through the crowd and came forward. Wayne introduced her to Earl.

"Did you pour this coffee for the actress?" Earl asked.

"I did, it came out of the coffee urn on our prop table." She replied.

136

"Is the urn still there and has anyone else drank from it?"

"Just about everyone in the crew has taken coffee from it, yes."

Earl asked her to take him to it, we followed. Earl opened the top of the urn and smelled, he said it was just coffee.

"Where did you get the cup from for the actress?"

Jane pointed to a stack of cups on the table and said from there. Earl lifted a cup and sniffed again. He stood looking puzzled.

"Okay, from this table to the set, cyanide got in the cup. Did you lose sight of the cup for any length of time and where was it?"

Jane looked upset and said, "I poured the coffee and took it to the desk by the computer and left it there, where the set dresser said to put it. I wasn't watching it and anyone could have gotten near it. There were so many people moving around getting the set ready and it could have happened anytime"

Earl thanked her and yelled to the crew standing around asking if anyone saw any person go near the cup of coffee. No one replied.

"Fine, we got another mystery." He turned to Howard Martin, who came in after Earl got there, "Howie, I don't want to shut down your production, but this is getting serious. We have to take all the intended victims of the original crime out of harms way until we can get a grip on this. Can you film around those scenes?"

"Well, yes," he said as he looked to Wayne and continued, "I guess we could eliminate those scenes from filming till later. How's that work for you Wayne?" Howard asked.

"I'm all for it, if it will help save a few lives for now, we can bunch the murder scenes together on one shooting day and watch the hell out of people." He said.

Earl said, "Well, since the killer has stated that he is after the intended murder victims, we'll take away his source. At least until we can get some evidence to find him."

I was standing next to Trapper and quietly asked if he had checked out Alice Stone's husband, he said he had planned on it later. I said it may be a good start. Earl heard me and asked what we were up to, so we told him and he got a look on his face that told me he wanted in on the chase.

"You think we should let the black ops boy in on our investigation?" I smiled to Trapper.

"Hey it's his case, he gets to drive." Trapper laughed. He filled Earl in on our plans.

Bob Moats

Earl called for his second in command and gave him instructions on questioning people again, and said he was going out to follow a lead. I went and told Penny and Tia what we were doing and they both bugged Earl about going. I could tell he wanted to impress Tia, so he relented and said they'd just have to stay out of the way.

Earl said he couldn't transport civilians in his cop car, so I offered to drive. Earl volunteered to sit in the back with the women; Trapper was quietly fighting him for the honor. We went out to my car and Trapper got to ride shotgun, he grumbled a bit about it.

I remembered where Alice Stone, aka Alice Morgan, and her husband lived, in Chesterfield Township, so I drove up and over to Gratiot, then up to where Buck, Deacon and I had talked to him when we were looking for Davey Morgan and Julia Waters, our two killers. We got there about a half hour later and pulled into the drive. Earl warned the women to stay in the car as he, Trapper and I went to the door. We rang the bell and a woman answered, I recognized her as the younger, second Alice, who was Alice Morgan, the name our killer Alice Stone took when she married Bob Morgan, this Alice's uncle. I moved forward and reminded her who I was.

"Oh, yes, I remember you, back when you were hunting down Davey and his crazy sister. Didn't you have something to do with their deaths?" She asked.

I was the one who shot Davey as he was threatening Penny with harm; it still haunted my dreams as I watched him die from my gun shots. "Yes, I was there when it happened, but we are investigating a new crime that may have something to do with Alice Stone, also know as Alice Morgan, your aunt. Is your uncle here by chance?"

She took on a sad look and said, "The reason I'm here is because I'm getting the contents of the house ready for auction. My Uncle Bob died about two months ago, I'm afraid he can't help you."

"May I ask how he died?" Earl spoke.

"He was so upset that Aunt Alice was killed that he took his own life. He started his car in the garage and never came out," she said as a tear formed in her eyes.

"I'm sorry for your loss, we won't bother you further." Earl said. We started to go when she called to me.

"I understand that they are doing a movie on the crime, is it going to have anything about my uncle?" She asked.

"It will mention him, yes, but I made sure it's being done tastefully, you have no worries about it." I offered.

She thanked me, then closed the door. I looked at Trapper and Earl saying, "I guess the crime doesn't die well does it."

"It never does." Trapper offered.

We went back to the car and Trapper slipped in the back seat quickly, grinning at Earl. He just quietly got in the front and I heard him mumble, I'll get him for that. Tia was loving every minute of it, she knew what was going on between the two men and was enjoying the rivalry. Penny just said for the two of them to grow up. I loved that girl.

I sat for a minute before starting the car. Earl asked if something was wrong.

"No, I was just trying to put things in perspective. Alice's husband is dead now two months, he would have been a prime candidate as killer, but now it's a dead end, pardon the pun. Davey and Julia were killed and so we have no more relatives to claim as killers."

Earl threw in, "Unless the younger Alice Morgan was mad about the death of her uncle and aunt and she's masterminding the whole thing."

"If you want to pursue that motive, be my guest, but I don't know if she could be involved. She wasn't even sure about the movie."

"Well, I'll keep her on my list, I have to, it's the detective's code of investigation." Earl laughed.

We drove back to the studio and Earl pulled all his men in and asked them of their findings, nothing was popping. He told them to go back to the precinct and he was staying around to observe. I knew better, the rivalry of the two men was just starting over Tia.

Made for TV Murders

Unfortunately for Earl, he got a call to get back to his precinct to finish writing up a report for another case he worked that was going to trial tomorrow, and the lawyers wanted the extra case details, he cussed quietly and said good-bye to everyone and left.

The crew had torn down sets not needed now and were working on a new set for the inside of Penny's home. I was amazed they did that, but I had asked the set designer about it, he said that they would have to be able to move walls to film from various angles for the camera and light placement, something they couldn't do in a real house. But exterior scenes would be filmed at Penny's.

I was studying the set when I saw a rather huge man in a Clinton Township police uniform and asked Trapper who that was.

"Ah, you weren't here this morning when they brought him in, that's the actor playing Deacon's part. I met him, nice guy, his name is Kurt Daniels. He's done a few TV shows, usually the bad guy because he is so big. I think he'll do Deacon justice."

I just nodded and called Penny over, since Tia had to go to make-up and wardrobe for her parts now being set up. I pointed out Deacon's double and Penny laughed at the resemblance. Wayne went to Kurt and brought him over to meet us.

"I'm pleased to meet you Kurt; you are a good likeness for Deacon." I said.

"Well, I just got in from Vegas yesterday, where I met with the real Deacon, he's quite a guy." He said.

"Then you met Lynn, too?" Penny asked.

"Yes, she said I could sub for Deacon anytime. I don't think the Deacon liked that."

"That sounds like Lynn." I said.

Someone called for Wayne and said they had the scene set for the dressing room at Penny's studio, where Jim and Penny meet again after forty years. I really wanted to see that. I tried to write in the script our roll in the hay as tasteful as possible, but this would be interesting. All the background and atmosphere actors were given their marks and herded around the set then they called for a take. Penny was holding on to my arm as we watched Leo Brooks, my actor and Tia go over the dressing room scenes. I noticed they filmed various scenes out of sequence that would be edited later to make sense.

Penny and I watched as Tia and Leo rolled around the place making out, it was a bit embarrassing to think everyone was watching. All the dressing room scenes were filmed up to the time when Penny found the killer's note on her dressing table and then they called in for Trapper and Deacon's first entrance to that part. I put into the script, the real comment I made about the feeding of the huge cops and they did it so well. All the filming went well and Wayne called for a dinner break, an hour, and be ready to get back to it.

I looked to Penny and asked if she wanted to go to the dressing room set and relive our first time having sex, she smiled and said she would think about it.

*

Chapter 21

Buck received a call back from Luther and he told Buck that he tracked down the tat that was on Steve's arm, it was from a defunct gang, Hell's Underground, that ran in Pontiac back in the late 80's. Most the members moved on after the death of a few members tore the group apart and no one was convicted for the killings. A few of the members, who the cops were still looking for, had slipped away. Buck wondered if Steve could be a wanted felon. He thanked Luther and then Luther told Buck he got a call from the movie casting director and they want his people to be in the movie, Buck said that was great and he would try and slip in with them, when they filmed.

Buck told Celeste what Luther had said and she worried if Steve was dangerous.

"Celeste, the guy puts a note on your door threatening to kill you if I stay here, I'd say he was dangerous."

144

Buck said. There was a knock on the door, Buck peeked through the hole and it was detective Handley. He opened the door and let him in.

"Hey Buck, any new developments?" he asked.

Buck told him about the tattoo and the connection with Hell's Underground and how he may be a wanted man. Handley said he'd get hold of mug shots of the gang members and show them to Celeste to see if he pops up. Buck said he was getting cabin fever and if the detective didn't have anything more important to do, he and Celeste could follow him to the precinct to look through his books. Handley smiled and said to stick close. They went out and drove to the Warren police precinct and into Handley's office. He said he'd have someone pull the mug books for Pontiac and they could look through them at their leisure.

About an hour later, Celeste came up with the photo of her stalker. His name was really Tony Marco, and a wanted man. Buck said he couldn't understand how this guy eluded the police for so long.

"Well, he probably laid real low, didn't get stopped by a cop and bought fake ID. It's been done before and will be done again." Handley spoke. "Okay, we need to watch your place and hope he returns. The warrant says he's wanted for murder, so we need to proceed with caution."

Celeste looked really distressed, thinking out loud, that she had slept with a killer, and she could have been killed. Buck told her not to think about it and he would be there for her.

Handley said, "It's a waiting game now, I'll have men watching, but be careful, we don't know how clever this guy is."

Buck thanked him and he and Celeste left the building. Buck took her for lunch at a Burger King, feeling fairly safe that Steve AKA Tony wasn't following. They got back to her apartment and went in, they got a surprise. The room had been vandalized and everything was thrown around. Buck pulled his .38 and checked the apartment to see if someone was still there, it was empty. He pulled his cell phone and called Handley and told him about the break-in.

~~*~~

Wayne had called for another take on the scene they just filmed; he felt it could be more intense. They had just filmed the late night attack by Davey Morgan in Penny's home. Leo did a good job being pinned behind the door being pushed by Davey's actor. Penny was fascinated by the re-creation of the crime, since she was hiding in the bathroom off the bedroom when it happened.

They had spent the better part of a day just working on a few scenes, it was a lengthy process for complicated scenes. The smaller, quicker scenes, with people just talking went smoothly and Wayne was happy with the progress. Howard came up to me, Penny and Trapper and was bubbling over the way things were going on the film.

"I have about fifteen extra security guards on hand so I hope that discourages the killer of the actresses." He added.

"Howard, the original killers murdered the women while the police were watching. We'll have to be really on our toes here." I warned.

"Yes, you're right; I just hope we get through this without any further incident. All the scenes with the murdered cheerleaders have been scheduled for later, and we aren't letting anyone know when. Just as a precaution." Howard smiled and said he had work to do and skittered off.

I looked to Penny and said, "Who does he remind you of."

Penny laughed and said, "Captain Weber." I heard Trapper laugh out loud at her statement and agreed.

Wayne was talking to Bill about location shoots and called Scott over to arrange for the transportation of the crew and equipment. Wayne came to us and said they were first going to Penny's home to film the outside shots and then to Buck's for the scenes there.

"I talked to Gloria and she talked to the original Luther about his biker group doing the background scenes at Buck's. Jim, can you let Buck know we will be there tomorrow afternoon?" Wayne asked.

"I'll call him shortly." I answered.

Tia came over and sidled up to Trapper and asked his opinion on the attack scene. Trapper was acting like an embarrassed schoolboy and told her he thought it did justice to the crime. I had to laugh because Trapper wasn't even there when it happened till later. She took his arm and asked if he wanted to go get some coffee and to tell her about crime fighting. They went off.

"This is going to be worth watching." I said to Penny. She smiled and said, "People can be so goofy when it comes to romance, or lust."

I told Penny I was calling Buck and we went outside to get away from all the construction noise. The phone rang a couple times and Buck answered. "Crime central," he spoke.

"The film company wants to start filming the scenes at your place tomorrow afternoon, so be ready, and how's your case going?" I asked.

Buck filled me in on everything that happened and said that Handley was back in the apartment now checking on the break-in with their CSU. "I doubt they will find anything since we know who did it, we just need to catch him now. I have an idea on something I'm going to try, then tomorrow we will both be at my place. What time are they coming?"

"Wayne just said tomorrow afternoon, you can bring Celeste, maybe we can slip her into the background too." I smiled.

"I think she'd like that. I'll have her and me at the house by ten o'clock and wait."

"It's a plan and still keep an eye out for Marco, he may follow you guys." I said.

"I hope he does, I really want to get my hands on this guy now." Buck replied and we finished.

I filled in Penny on the situation with Buck just as Tia and Trapper came back. I told him about Buck and he said he'd have to call Handley to get his opinion.

Wayne called Tia back to film a couple close-ups of her and my actor in the living room. She excused herself from Trapper and went off. I looked at Trapper and laughed.

"You aren't the marrying type and she would never settle for a cop as a husband." I commented.

"I didn't say I wanted to get married, she could just take me on as a gigolo, I could get used to the high life," he smiled.

"You a gigolo? That's a laugh." Penny said.

Made for TV Murders

"Penny, be fair, Trapper was a great pimp out in Vegas, he has the experience to handle loose women." I said seriously. Trapper just gave us the finger and walked away. "Do you think I offended him?" I laughed.

I was watching the people getting the set ready when I felt someone tap on my shoulder, I jumped. It was Wendell, sneaking up on me again.

"Wendell, I swear I'm going to put a bell on you, stop creeping up behind me."

"Sorry, Mr. Richards. I was asked to give you this." He said as he handed me an envelope. "It came in through the mail to the front office. The receptionist asked me to give it to you." He smiled and walked back to his post at the door.

I looked at the envelope and there was no return address, just my name and the address here at the studio. Trapper came back to me after seeing the security guard hand me the envelope. He asked what I got.

"It's addressed to me, I need to open it to find out what it is, may I?"

"By all means, lets see who your fans are, or if the killer is writing you now." Trapper smiled.

I carefully tore open the envelope and handled the inner folded sheet of paper by the edges, so I didn't mess up any fingerprints. I unfolded the letter and read out loud.

"Jim Richards, you are one of the people who has torn out my heart. Your interference in matters you shouldn't have gotten into make me want to strike out to those who symbolize the hurt I am going through and especially those persons who took the love of my life away. I will strike out and you will not be able to stop me. Kiss your precious wife good-bye, she's the last cheerleader, and I'll even take out that woman pretending to be her. Your buddy Trapper is especially going to die. This movie will not be finished and people will not know of the false accusations against my love. I will succeed, so be aware."

I looked at Trapper and said, "You want to call Earl, or should I?"

*

Chapter 22

"Okay, this is admitting that the new killer is definitely attached to Alice Stone, Julia Waters and Davey Morgan. I'm calling in Alice Morgan to interview her and see where she fits in this. Anyone else you guys know of for a connection to the original crime?" Earl asked.

Made for TV Murders

We were sitting in a conference room, Trapper, Penny with Willy, Earl and I. Tia was doing a few more scenes for Wayne and even though she was singled out in the letter also, we didn't want to alarm her. Or I should say Earl didn't want to alarm her.

"Do we know that Bob Morgan is actually dead, just on Alice Morgan's word?" I asked.

"Yeah, I checked on his death, he was found in his garage, carbon monoxide poisoning. I read the coroner's report after I got back to the office. Nice to have everything on computer now days." Earl sat back and stared at the note, now in a plastic sleeve that I got from the receptionist. CSU wasn't called; Earl said he'd take the letter in to the lab to recover any prints.

Earl looked at the envelope; he suddenly made a face and asked me, "You say this was delivered by mail here?"

"That's what Wendell said, it came to the lobby and the receptionist asked him to bring it to me." I replied.

"Strange, because this letter wasn't canceled by the Post Office. It's got squiggle marks on the stamp, but they look like they were done by hand with a marker. Let's go see the receptionist." Earl stood and we followed him out to the front lobby. The red-head who I met the first day I came to the building was there. Earl went to her and flashed his badge; the girl smiled and said she already knew he was a cop.

"Did you receive this letter in the mail today?" He asked showing her the envelope.

"It was in with the pile of mail that was on the counter when I got back from lunch. I didn't see the mail person actually drop it off." She replied.

Earl thought on that for a second, "How long where you gone for lunch and did anyone watch the lobby for you."

"Well, I asked one of the security guards to keep an eye out and then I went to lunch."

"Which guard?" Earl asked.

"He was a tall, young guy, his name tag said, George Lester."

"Is he still here?"

"I guess so, he came out here to check on the lobby and before he went off I asked him if he could watch the place, he said he would."

Earl thanked her and we went to the soundstage, stopping at Wendell's desk and Earl asked if he knew where George Lester was. Wendell said that George left for the day and said he was going home. Earl asked if Wendell knew where George lived, Wendell told him he didn't. Earl asked him to get on the phone and call his bosses to find out. Wendell did.

Made for TV Murders

Earl turned to Trapper and me and said this letter didn't come in the mail; it was dropped here by the killer. That means he was or is in this building, maybe a worker, actor or even a guard. I looked at Wendell and couldn't imagine this slow, old man strangling the first woman; he would have been knocked on his ass if he tried.

Wendell wrote something on a paper and brought it to Earl. Earl said that he was going to check on this guard, I said I'd drive if we could go along. He asked if Tia was around, I laughed and said she was busy acting. He frowned and said that we could go. We went to my Crown Vic and drove out to Highland Park, not far from the studio and we found the address of George Lester. Earl led Trapper and me, leaving Penny to the safety of the car, and went to the door. Earl rang the doorbell.

A tired looking man opened the door and Earl showed him his badge asking if he was George Lester, the man said he was and Earl identified himself saying he wanted to ask a few questions. The man asked what it was about.

"You watched the lobby at the studio this morning for the receptionist while she went to lunch, is that correct?" Earl asked.

"Yeah, I sat for about thirty minutes watching till she got back, why?" He said.

"Did the mail arrive while you were at the front desk?"

"Yeah, a couple minutes after the receptionist left," he replied.

"Did anyone go near the mail after it arrived?"

"There were so many people coming and going in the lobby, a lot of people were near the mail, why?" He was looking confused.

"Okay George, we have a piece of mail that didn't come in with the mail that was delivered, it was put on the pile. Did you see anyone drop an envelope on the pile?" Earl asked.

"As I said there were a lot of people milling about, I wasn't watching the mail that carefully. Anyone could have done it."

"Do you remember who was in the lobby while you were there?"

"I remember a few people; I'm new to the building so I'm not real familiar with the people who worked there. I can give you a few names."

"Great, can you write them down for me?" Earl asked and George said he would. Earl told us he would go in to get the list, we could wait outside. I turned to see Penny holding up Willy so he could watch me, I waved and he started squiggling and yipping. I told Trapper that I was going back to the car and he followed. We sat for a bit and then Earl came out to the car.

"Not a big list, George said he didn't know many people but this is something we can start with." Earl said. "I also asked him a few more questions; he's not on my radar. He only started working there yesterday morning."

"May I see the list?" I asked and he handed it to me. I read over the short list and it was mostly the production people and two guards, one was Wendell. I handed the list back and headed back to the studio.

"Jim, you worked for a security company, do they do a good check on their hires?" Earl asked.

"The company I worked for said they did a thorough background check, but they told me a number of lies while I was there, so I didn't trust them. I can't speak for other companies."

"Well, there were two guards in the lobby; one was your buddy Wendell. I'll talk to him and the other guard first so not to disturb the film company." Earl said.

We arrived at the studio and Earl went to Wendell at this desk and asked if he could talk, he said yes and we went to the conference room and sat.

"Wendell, how are you doing today?" Earl asked.

Bob Moats

Wendell looked cool and comfortable and replied he was fine. He kept eye contact with Earl as they spoke.

"Wendell, how long have you worked for Ever Vigilant Security?"

"About three weeks, I joined just before they started guarding here."

"What did you do before that?"

"I was retired from General Motors; I was a designer for almost 30 years. Got tired of sitting home and this is an easy job. Well, it was until the murders, terrible thing."

"Yes, it was. Were you in the lobby earlier today while George Lester was watching the desk?"

"Yes, I was wondering what happened to him, he went out there and didn't come back. I was put in charge of the guards by my boss and I didn't want anyone being lazy. I found that he was watching the lobby for Janice, the receptionist, and I went back to my desk." he said calmly and smiled.

"Wendell, Jim said you read his book, did you know of the crime or people in the book before you read it?"

"I had heard about it on the TV back when it first happened and they made a big deal out of it. I bought and read the book to see what it was all about and I heard they were going to make a movie out of it. One reason I was interested in working for this company, to see it being filmed."

"Okay, Wendell, thank you for your time, you can go back to work, and would you find and send in Terry Fenton for me?" Earl asked.

"Sure Detective, I'll track him down for you." Wendell said and left the room.

"The guy is an old, wet noodle; he wouldn't have the strength to murder any of the women. He sat at a desk for years, getting no exercise. I hope the next guard is big and in better shape." Earl said.

A few minutes later another guard came it. He was big and in better shape, he was an African-American in his late twenties, tall, about 230 pounds and looked like a body builder by the muscles that stretched his guard shirt. Earl asked him to sit.

"Your name is Terry Fenton?"

"Yep, it is." he said quickly.

"You were in the lobby today while George Lester was watching it, correct?"

"Yep, I went to see where George had gone off to, we were supposed to be watching the film crew. I thought he might be goofing off."

"Did you see a pile of mail on the lobby counter while you were out there?"

"Nope, I was busy talking to George, I didn't see any pile."

"What do you know of the murders that occurred here this week?"

"Just what my bosses told me, I didn't get here till yesterday, so I didn't see what happened."

"Where were you earlier in the week?"

"I was guarding around the MGM Grand casino downtown. I'd rather be there than here though, more beautiful women."

Earl just went quiet and told him to go back to work. He smiled and left.

Earl turned to me, grinned and said, "I was hoping the killer would be a rent-a-cop."

*

Chapter 23

Buck and Celeste rested after cleaning the apartment from the vandalism that Tony had done. Celeste looked like she was going to break down and cry; Buck felt bad and then mad.

"Hey, this guy is going to get caught, he will fuck up and we'll catch him. So stop worrying and nothing is going to harm you while I'm around. Can you do that for me?" Buck asked.

She looked to him and smiled, "I know you will, I'm so glad you're here."

"Well, tomorrow we're going back to my place and they are coming to start filming the movie scenes there. I'll even slip you into the background of the movie and maybe you'll be discovered as a star." He laughed.

"Thanks Buck, I appreciate it." She said quietly.

There was a knock on the door, Buck went and peeked through the hole, then looked to Celeste and smiled, "My posse is here." He opened the door and there stood Luther. They greeted each other and then about six other men walked up behind Luther, all wearing their biker colors. Buck called Celeste over and introduced everyone, explaining that she is the victim that he's protecting. Buck asked Boon if he could guard

Celeste while he took the rest of the guys outside for a reconnoiter. Boon said he would and Buck led Luther and the others down to the front door of the building, stopping just inside.

"Okay, there is some psycho stalking Celeste and the cops and I believe that he could be watching the place. I'll tell the cops who are on surveillance out there, what we're doing, I want you guys to spread around and look for someone just sitting watching the place. Don't get in trouble; just yell if you find anyone. Okay, spread out."

They hit the front door and went off in different directions. Buck went over to the unmarked cop car down the road and explained that they would be looking around for Tony for a short while and would yell if they find anything. The cop in the driver seat said for them to be careful and they would be waiting for anything.

Buck went back to the apartment front door again and stood listening.

Earl had gone through George's list of people who were in the lobby where the mail was sitting. He sat back in his chair and frowned, "I'm not getting anything off these people. Do we have a Phantom of the movie studio? Someone lurking in the shadows doing this damage? I don't know, I'm going to go pull in Alice Morgan and see what I can get from her. You guys be on your toes here, I'll call back later and let you know what I find."

Made for TV Murders

Earl stood and went out the door, I looked at Trapper and said, "Shall we go out and observe our actors?" Trapper and Penny followed me out and we went back to the studio, Wendell was at the door to the studio and asked if we found out anything. I told him we were still investigating and I'd let him know.

Tia had finished her scenes and came over when she saw us. Trapper moved closer toward her and puffed out his chest, I was waiting for him to thump his chest like a gorilla, he didn't. She got closer to him than she needed to be and I was trying to hold back a laugh when Trapper's face got a little red. Penny whispered in my ear that this was getting silly, I agreed.

"So what have you people been up to, I saw you all running around pulling people in to the conference room, something happening?" She asked.

"Well, we did get another letter from the killer, and we have a bit more info on his motives." Trapper offered, trying to sound official.

Tia got her face up close to Trappers and asked if it had anything to do with her. He looked like he would keel over that she was so close and said, "Well, the note did mention you were in danger, but I'm going to be sticking close to make sure you're safe."

Tia put her arm around Trapper's shoulder now and said in his ear, closely, "Thank you so much, I appreciate all your efforts."

Bob Moats

I was waiting for Trapper to break out in a sweat, just as Tia moved away and said she had to change for the day, they were finished filming for now. She flashed her eyes at Trapper and asked if he wanted to help her change. He stood looking shocked, and she laughed and ran off. He just stood there like a deer in headlights.

"I remember when you asked me that in your dressing room that first day. I didn't get to help you change either." I said to Penny.

"That's because you weren't fast enough, I would have let you." She laughed and went off after Tia. Trapper and I just stood looking at each other, I said, "We're pathetic aren't we?" He nodded.

Buck heard a yelling from down the street opposite from the unmarked car, then a gun shot. Buck waved to the cops, but they were already aware of the sound. They started up their car and sped down to where Buck was heading. About three of Buck's friends were standing by a car, the driver door open, it was empty.

Buck asked, "What happened?" The tallest of the men said, "Benny and I creeped up behind this car that someone was sitting in and then we startled him. He pulled a gun on us and we spread out and ducked. He fired once and got out, I guess to try and finish us off, when he saw you and the cop car coming. I think he was trying to decide to get back to the car or run, he ran."

163

Made for TV Murders

The cop stood looking around the neighborhood and said that it was starting to get too dark out to track him, but we had his car and he would have to be on foot now.

"Thanks for being cautious about firing back, guys, but I'm sure none of you are armed, are you?" The cop smiled and went back to his car to call the incident in.

Buck grinned at Luther and they all went back to the apartment. "Well, we got him thinking now." Buck said as they got to Celeste's door and went in after Boon opened it for them.

Tia and Penny came out from the dressing room after a bit, as Trapper and I sat on a couple of chairs on the dressing room set. The actor playing Deacon was sitting with us and he stood as the women came over. I looked at Trapper and said that he was polite wasn't he. Just like Deacon, Trapper said.

We all decided to call it a night and head back to the house. Penny smiled and asked Trapper and the fake Deacon of they wanted to join us. They both said they'd like that. Kurt said that was nice, since he didn't know anyone around here. We were just heading out when Earl came flying back in.

"I didn't miss anything, did I?" He said breathless.

"Nope, we were just going home, care to join us?" I offered.

"Well, if it's not too much trouble, sure." He smiled at Tia and offered her a ride; she smiled and said she was good to go with me and Penny, but thanks.

We started out and I said to Earl quietly, "Nice try." He stuck out his tongue and we went to our cars, Kurt went with Trapper.

After stopping to get a few refreshments, we arrive at our home. We sat for most the evening and talked about the day and then I asked Earl if he questioned Alice Morgan.

"Yep, she was real nice, I felt like a creep asking her questions about her dead uncle and her activities for the last week, she was so sickly sweet and cooperative. I found out that there are no more Morgans around other than herself. She's divorced and retained her maiden name, she's the last Morgan in her line. It was just her and her uncle left. That's sad."

"Well, she could get pregnant and have a son that would carry on the name." Trapper offered.

"Are you offering?" Earl smirked.

"I was just saying, not volunteering." Trapper said.

Tia was sitting between the two cops on the couch and I could tell she was amused by it. They kept looking over to her and then to the other man, probably hoping he would go home.

Around 11 P.M. Tia stretched and said she was tired and was going to bed, since she had a full day of shooting tomorrow. Besides she had to study her lines, and she likes to do that in bed. She stood and thanked everyone for the pleasant talk; she bent down and kissed each man on the cheek, thanking them for the protection, and then went to the guestroom. Earl and Trapper looked at each other, then they each made their apologies and said they should be going. We let them go and Earl took our fake Deacon with him, Kurt said he had a nice time. We said anytime and they left.

Penny and I plopped down on the couch and Willy climbed up on my lap and dropped. I looked at Penny and said this is getting both fun and complicated.

"Yes, sweetie, my life with you is always a joy. Between murder and crazy friends, I have it all." She kissed my nose and went off to the bedroom, looking back to me and asking if I wanted to help her undress. I didn't need to think about it twice, I went.

*

Chapter 24

Buck thanked Luther and his friends, as they left and said he'd see them tomorrow at his house for the filming of the movie. He turned to Celeste and said that she should pack a bag because she may need to stay at his place for a day or two since Tony probably would be on the prowl now, but the cops can watch for him. She went off to her bedroom to pack as Buck pulled his cell phone to call me. I was busy with Penny so I let the call go to voicemail. Buck quickly left an explanation of the events of the night and that he and Celeste were going to be at his house and would see us tomorrow. He hung up and then helped Celeste take her bags out to his car and they headed to his home.

Penny had gone off to the kitchen to grab a couple of beers for her and I, then returned to the bedroom. I said I had her trained well; she stood for a moment at the foot of the bed and then set my beer on the dresser. She climbed in under the covers and said I could get my own beer. I just looked at her, then grumbled as I got out of the bed and went to the dresser. I got back under the covers and laid back.

"I think I'll get one of those cube refrigerators so we don't have to keep going to the kitchen." I said.

Made for TV Murders

She looked at me for a moment or two, then said, "I'm going to have to start you on an exercise program; you're getting to be a lazy old fart."

"Doesn't sex count as exercise?" I asked.

She stared at me again for a bit then said, "Not the way you do it." She hit the remote and turned on the TV and laid back watching a movie as I tried to think of a good come back. I couldn't, so I just drank my beer and grinned.

The next morning Penny had to go to work, so she was getting ready to go. I told Tia that I would take her to Buck's for the filming and she said that would be good for her. Wayne called shortly after and said they were coming to our home to film a couple outside scenes in the backyard and then they would be at Buck's for the rest of the outdoor scenes for today. Penny had gone off and I was in the kitchen getting Willy his breakfast. Willy and Tia had become good pals and were playing on the couch when there was a knock at the front door. Tia said she would get it and went to check, it was Trapper. She let him in and went back to the couch as Trapper watched her and Willy play some more. I put Willy's bowl on the floor, and Willy heard it hit, he stormed into the kitchen as I went to the living room.

"Will, don't you have criminals to chase?" I asked.

"I took a little time off to be technical advisor on the film for my parts and for proper police procedures. My captain said he was happy I was taking the time for the film, I think he was glad I was doing it and not just because I was gone from the station." He laughed as he sat on the couch next to Tia.

"Dream on, oh wise one." I smiled. "Today they have to film a couple scenes out back and then to Buck's place for the rest of the day. You weren't at any of those places as I remember, so you may as well go back to work."

He did a sideways glance at Tia and said, "No problem, I want to be around to guard Tia, so she comes to no harm."

Tia looked at him, smiled and gave him a kiss on the cheek. "Thank you so much for your concern, I appreciate it."

I said I had to go get ready for the day, "You two behave there, I don't want to have to yell at you." I went to the bathroom to clean up and to the bedroom to put on some decent clothes. I got back to the living room and Tia was chattering to Will about her trips around the world. I saw out the front window a couple of huge trucks pulling in. I went to the front porch and greeted Wayne as he came up.

"Jim, good morning! Hope everything is well with you?" He beamed brightly. "Nice weather."

"It's a good day to shoot, unusual for Michigan." I laughed and invited him in. He shook Trapper's hand

and gave Tia a hug and a kiss. I asked if he had breakfast and he said he didn't eat breakfasts, messes with his stomach too early in the day. I knew that feeling. We talked a bit about what was going on outside and then the actors who played our parts came knocking at the door. Wayne greeted them and we all sat in the living room going over the scenes to be shot here. Wayne and I then led everyone out to the backyard where the crew had set up lights, cameras and props and Wayne ran everyone through their paces. It took about two hours for the filming here then Wayne said he was happy and we could move to Buck's place.

I went to the side of the circus and called Buck. He came on sounding happy, "Jimmy, there's all kinds of activity going on here. Two trucks rolled in about an hour ago and all these people started getting the place ready to shoot. Luther and the guys are all here, it's like old times, when you coming?"

"We just finished shooting here and are heading there; you'll finally get to meet your alter-ego, the clone Buck." I laughed, "Anything more on your stalker?"

"Nope, it's been quiet since me and the boys scared him off last night. Besides we got enough fire power here to blast him to hell and back if he shows his face here."

"Well, let the police have the biggest pieces first, then you can have what's left. See you shortly"

"Great, see you when you get here." He said and hung up.

I was walking around the side of the house going up to get the car ready to take Tia and me to Buck's when I nearly ran into Earl. "What are you doing here, as if I had to ask?"

"I just came by to see if everything was going well on the filming and there are no more murders." He smiled.

"So, how is your investigation going?"

"Absolutely nowhere. We got zip on any forensics and no more emails to go by; even the earlier ones were untraceable. This guy is playing for time now, till the film people start to shoot the murder scenes again. But we'll be watching. If we can get through those scenes without him succeeding in murdering anyone, it will mess up his plans."

"Yeah, but if that happens maybe he will get desperate and do some damage elsewhere." I offered.

"Well, as long as he does no harm to Tia, and of course Penny, we are good. Not that I want anyone dead, but we have to protect the important persons." He smiled.

Tia came around the house with Trapper; Earl gave a nasty look to Trapper who just smiled back. "Hey Earl, how's crime in Detroit?"

Made for TV Murders

"Better than in Clinton Township, shouldn't you be fighting crime there?" Earl came back.

"Nope, got time off to guard our little star here and to make sure they do my part right." He smiled back as Earl gritted his teeth. I hoped this didn't end up in a fist fight.

"Okay, you two, we have to go to Buck's, so let's play nice and get over there." I said. I could see Tia was really enjoying the attentions from the men, she was such a tease.

Earl and Trapper tried to get Tia to go with each of them to Buck's, but she laughed and said she was going to go with me. I felt sorry for them both, they looked crushed. Tia and I went back into the house to gather our things and I packed Willy into his purse and slung him over my shoulder. We walked out past Earl and Trapper and went to my Crown Vic and headed out as the men ran to their cars to follow. Trapper knew where Buck lived, but Earl didn't, so I figured Trapper would try to lose Earl on the roads.

We arrived to Buck's and they had the motorcycles and their riders sitting in the lot next to Buck's property for the big parade onto the property. They had the cameras, lights and equipment set up and ready to go. All the actors gathered at Buck's front porch and were introduced to Buck. He walked up to Vince Morris, the actor playing him and they both smiled that walrus smile to each other and then Buck turned his head to me and said, "I approve!" He shook Vince's hand and they went off to talk, Vince wanted to pick Buck's brain for the incidents of the crime.

I turned to see Trapper drive in, park, and when he came over I asked what took him so long to get here. He smiled and said, "I had to drive all over the damn place to lose Earl. If he calls, don't tell him where we are."

*

Chapter 25

About three minutes later Earl roared in and parked; he came storming over and I thought he was going to punch Trapper. "Thanks, dipwad, but you didn't lose me. Nice try though." He grinned and punched Trapper in the arm, hard. Trapper winced but wouldn't show pain in front of Tia. I was still loving watching this rivalry.

Wayne called for Tia and got all the principle actors together for a bull session. He plotted out the shooting schedule for the rest of the day and what parts everyone was in. The crew had everything ready to go and then Wayne called for action and signaled Luther for his cue, so they rode their motorcycles and three hot rods on to the property as the cameras rolled. I remembered the first day they did this, it was chilling to see again. Buck had called his friends in to help protect Penny from Julia and Davey, and afterwards the gang had treated

Made for TV Murders

Penny like a queen. They even started her first fan club, with Luther as president and a girl called Mouse as vice-president. The filming of the entrance scene by the bikes and cars was completed and they filmed the introductions of Luther and his people to our lead players. The group started to put up the tents and camping things like they did back then, as cameras filmed the set-up.

Wayne called for a break and everyone hit the hoagie wagon that Howard had hired to feed everyone. I asked Wayne how he was feeling about the shoot so far.

"I'm very happy with it all, I'm sure when I see the dailies, I'll have a better grip on it, but I think they will be fine." he replied and went off to talk to the cinematographer.

I was now standing with Becker who came with a patrol car for the scenes with the clone Deacon, compliments of the Clinton Township Police to be used for filming. Barry was not in any of the scenes anymore, but was thrilled with the one's he was in. "How are you doing with your magic?" I asked, remembering the events of our trip to the magic convention a few months back.

"I've been practicing every chance I get, I still remember Marty's advice to me, I sure miss him." Becker said.

"So do I, but I'm sure Marty is watching over all us and would be proud of what you have done so far.

When we are finished with the film, I'll have everyone over to our house for a wrap party and you can perform." I said as he beamed at me.

Just as we were talking, Penny drove in and parked; she must have finished work for the day and came to join us. She bounced over and latched on to me with a big wet kiss. Probably trying to annoy Trapper and Earl since they were still hoping for a break from Tia. I told her she was being cruel, she said she knew that and smiled evilly. She waved to Tia and then smiled at Trapper and Earl, saying how nice the day was, so spring like, romance is in the air. I realized that Penny had a definite mean streak in her if she wanted, luckily she never used it on me.

Wayne had a number of takes filmed after we finished with lunch and then we were taking a short break while the crew set up another shot for the kidnapping of Penny. It came later in the story but everything was being filmed out of order while they had the use of Buck's property. I finally got a chance to talk to the actress who was playing Julia Waters, she had an uncanny resemblance to the crazy serial killer, it was a bit unnerving. She told me she had read my book and it provided a bit of details on the woman's psychological profile. I just thought Julia was nuts.

The filming went well as the actors playing Julia and Davey took Penny hostage and left the property. My real Penny wasn't feeling up to watching the events of the kidnapping, the memories of the original crime still gave her occasional nightmares that I had to deal with late at night. The car with the killers and Tia drove back onto the property after they were filmed escaping and they got out of the car and came to Wayne for further instructions. They filmed the scenes of the motorcycles and their riders all heading out to chase the killers, then they returned to the property. Later when it got darker they would film down the road at the real bar where the good guys waited for Davey to show. They received permission to shoot there, that made the bar owners very happy.

Penny pulled me aside and said, "My producer said the film company had called the studio and got permission to film in the studio this week. Of course he wanted a credit at the end saying it was filmed at the studio and he wanted Lonie to have her crew film the whole thing for my show."

"Your producer sure likes to film things, maybe he should go into documentaries." I laughed. I looked over to Earl and Trapper playing nice, sitting on Buck's lawn chairs and watching Tia go through her paces.

I took Willy's purse off and told Penny she could take care of our baby for a while. She took the leash from the pocket of the purse and hooked him up, then walked around with him. Penny's biker fan club including Luther and Mouse came over to greet her and admire Willy. He was a little unsettled by the group but once they gave him attention he begged for more.

Buck came to me with Celeste and I asked her how she was doing. "I'm good today, Buck and I walked around in the background of the camp while they filmed, I'm so amazed that I'll be in a movie. Even if it's a tiny part." I realized that I forgot to get in the scene myself; I'd have to rectify that later.

"Anything on Marco, or has he been frightened away by your gang?" I smiled.

"Haven't heard anything, I gave Handley my cell number in case they run into him. Heard nothing so far."

"There's no way he could have followed you here?"

"Not unless he stole another car, he was on foot last night when my boys chased him away." Buck smiled. Luther came up and asked Celeste how she was holding up; she thanked him for helping last night. He said it was his pleasure.

We were standing there as Boon came up and said, "You know something strange is happening. Remember back when you asked us to watch for anything or anyone suspicious around the property and Davey was watching?" We nodded. "Well there's someone back in the bushes again where Davey was hiding, I just saw him as I went to park my bike."

I looked over to the property where Davey was last spotted and saw nothing, but I told Buck and Luther that we needed a repeat of the last time. I called Trapper and Earl, they came over and I explained what we were going to do. Trapper called Becker and told him on our cue, to drive the patrol car on the road to the left and block anyone coming out of the property next to us. Becker strolled to the car and sat in the driver seat waiting.

"This may be nothing but a curiosity seeker watching us, but it could be Tony Marco. Let's see if we can take him." I said and Buck and Luther strolled out the driveway to the road and when they were at the shoulder of the road I signaled to Becker, he drove out and everyone ran towards the lot. Becker saw a car parked off the side and pulled up in front of it, just as a man came storming out of the property. Becker jumped out with gun drawn just as Buck and Luther came up. The man pulled a gun and ducked behind the parked car and started firing. He managed to open the car door and get in as Trapper and Earl were firing on him. He got the car started and rammed the patrol car allowing him the room to drive off. We fired a bit more but he was getting away. Trapper ran to the patrol car but saw the front tire had been bent by the car crash, it wasn't going anywhere without a tow. Becker got on the car radio and called New Baltimore police to watch for the car.

I looked at everyone and yelled, "Didn't anyone think to shoot out his tires!" Penny wasn't going to let us forget this, maybe she wouldn't notice.

I looked down the road back toward Buck's drive and saw Wayne with a cameraman holding a Steadicam, filming the whole thing. I thought, oh great, something to remember our screw-up by.

Chapter 26

We all went back up to the house, as the New Baltimore cops came driving in, Earl and Trapper told them what was going on and they said they'd watch for the car after Trapper gave the cop a description of the car. Buck gave him a copy of the picture of Marco that Handley provided him and they drove off. Trapper was going to call for a tow for the police car, but Wayne said that they had a crew that could fix the car; he called on his walkie-talkie and told someone to take care of it. He smiled and said they fix cars all the time for movies, to reuse them.

Penny came to me with a big shit-eating grin. I stopped her and said, "Don't say it; you were right about the tire shooting thing. Even I didn't think about it and I got off a couple shots at the car. It should be in the manual." I tried to look happy.

"I forgive you, but now everyone is jumpy after hearing the gun fire going on so close. Well, it didn't bother the bikers, but the crew is not happy. Between the murders at the studio and gun play out here, no wonder they're scared." Penny was holding Willy tightly; he looked to me for help so I took him from her.

Wayne came over, he was excited and said he wished he could put the footage into the film, but it wasn't part of the original story. They went back to filming to get moving and to take everyone's minds off crime and

179

danger. By 6:30 they had filmed all the principle scenes at Buck's and the crew was packing everything as a second unit crew was setting up down at the Bore's Head bar for the filming there. My little posse and I went down to watch the filming and when it was in the can, Wayne called it a night.

Trapper's cell phone rang and it was his friend Handley asking about the activities that Buck had called him about. Trapper filled him in on his take of what happened. Handley warned that Marco was now making this a vendetta, so to be careful and then finished the call. Trapper told Buck what Handley said and asked if Buck wanted Becker to hang around, Buck said his friends would provide extra protection, but thanked him for his concern.

Penny made a comment about having everyone over for another party, but she didn't sound excited about it. Tia said she was tired and wanted to get some rest, so Earl and Trapper took the hint and said they'd see us tomorrow back at the studio. They left together, followed by Becker in the quickly restored patrol car, the movie mechanics were fast. I was sure Earl and Trapper were watching to see if the other would sneak back, but I took Tia and Penny to my car and we left after saying good-bye to Buck and Celeste. Luther and his people were going to continue camping since they were all set up for it. They already had a fire going in the pit.

Before we left the property I said to Penny, "Does this look familiar to you? A nut job is after Celeste and she is being guarded by Buck and his boys."

"Yep, it's a repeat; I hope it turns out better than my abduction."

We drove to our home and happily there was no one waiting in the drive. We went into the house and Penny said she was going to take an intensive spin on the stripper pole to help tire her out to sleep. Tia said that sounded like a good idea and they both went off to the porch. I looked down at Willy standing by me, I was sure he was hungry since he only had a few bites of a sub from the hoagie truck, I smiled at him and he followed me to the kitchen. I gave him a big bowl of food, which he ate without taking a breath. I raided the fridge and finally settled on ham slices and cheese on a Kaiser roll and a cold beer, just as the girls came back in. They looked deliciously sweaty and both raced to the bathroom for the shower. I was hoping they would take one together and invite me, but they didn't. Oh well.

I went to my desk on the porch and from under it I pulled out a lunch cooler that was big enough to hold six cans of beer and filled it from the fridge. I took it to the bedroom and Penny was in there drying her hair with a towel.

"Did you girls enjoy your shower, did you scrub each others backs?" I asked.

Made for TV Murders

"You'll never know, just enjoy the fantasy, and yes we did." She gave me her evil grin.

I just stared at her and put the cooler on the bed stand next to my side. Penny asked what it was for and I reminded her of the beer incident last night, I was ready now, I brought my own and she can get her exercise getting her own. She dove for the cooler as I was undressing and grabbed a beer out of it, yelling its community property. I just gave in and told her to enjoy it.

We snuggled and watched TV till we wore out; it was early but a long day. Willy was sleeping peacefully on his Bate's motel chair and shortly Penny was sound asleep. I just laid there thinking about the day and the crossing of crimes between Buck's case and the movie murders. Since I became a P.I., murders just seemed to be part of the deal. I just had to remember to keep my head down and aim my gun carefully. I fell asleep shortly after.

Next morning, Penny and Tia were busy getting beautiful and I struggled out of bed to take a shower. I lathered up thinking about the chances of a threesome, but knew it was just a dream, but a nice one. I dried off and dressed, finding Tia at the snackbar eating toast, Penny had gone off to work, Tia said she took Willy with her.

"Are we going to have any more excitement today?" Tia asked.

"I certainly hope not. I'm not happy about you or Penny around all this activity. Not much I can do, but just keep an eye on both of you."

"Well, I thank you for that. Besides I have two protecting angels watching over me now." She gave me an evil Penny smile. I laughed.

"Doesn't it bother you that they both have a crush on you?"

"Oh hell no, I love it. I won't string them along, besides I'm married, but do not repeat that to anyone. I married a great man about a year ago, and we have kept it secret, so the press wouldn't hound us. It's known that we live together but the wedding was a real feat to keep under cover."

"I guess so, I never heard about it. Actually you haven't done anything to entice Trapper and Earl, so you've been a good girl."

"And I plan on staying that way. I have an old ethic about marriage, I value it. So does John, my husband, he's a veterinarian in Santa Barbara where we live. He's okay with me being the star, he's a quiet person and very loving, we get along like you and Penny do, I admire your relationship."

"Thank you, I have a devotion to Penny, I feel we're soul mates." I smiled and ate the last bite of the toast I had made while talking. We got ourselves ready to go and headed out to the car.

Made for TV Murders

We arrived at the studio and I dropped Tia off at the door and parked. I was just coming up to the building when Trapper and Becker came up from their car.

"Good morning, is your captain letting both of you hang around here now?" I asked.

"Yep, he was happy to get rid of both of us." Trapper laughed. "I justified it by saying the reputation of the Clinton Township police was at stake and I wanted to be sure we were represented properly."

"You haven't changed have you, still full of it." We went in and were greeted by Wendell, standing at his door. "No murders while we were gone, Wendell?

"Nope, Mr. Richards, all quiet." He replied.

Wayne was talking to Scott Bailey, probably plotting the next move. Wayne saw me and excused himself from Scott and came over.

"Jim, good morning, and you too Will, Barry." He said as he shook everyone's hands. The guy was definitely friendly.

"What's the schedule looking like today?" I asked.

"The second unit crew will be filming on the freeway for the chase scenes; we got the state police helping too. We'll be going to the TV studio, some of the crew is already there setting up and Bill is mapping out the location for me. I'm going to put you through your paces today to guide me through the building."

"No problem, it's still burned into my memory so we should have no problems, as long as the studio is cooperative."

"They've given us carte blanche for filming. Penny's producer, Gordy, told me he would have the areas we needed cleared out of people, since most of the scenes took place in the back of the studio, so we're good to go." He got called away by someone and excused himself.

"Well, you're on your own then, I wasn't at the studio till after all the killing was over." Trapper said.

Earl came strolling up and said good morning. I said, "Earl, I'm going to ask you the same thing I asked Trapper, don't they miss you at your precinct?"

He smiled and said, "I'll tell you the same thing Trapper always says, I'm a lieutenant, I assign people to do things then hide. Actually this is still an active open murder investigation so I assigned myself to it."

Tia came walking over to the men and they both gushed, I wanted so badly to tell them about Tia being married, but I promised I wouldn't say anything about it. Damn, I wanted to take the wind out of their sails.

*

Chapter 27

Everyone was assembled at Penny's studio and there was a good number of station staff watching from the sides. Penny had just finished her show and came out of the studio and found me standing with the bad-boy twins. She greeted Earl and Trapper and asked if they didn't have crime to fight, they both grunted and ignored her, she smiled.

"The station is all jumping about the filming and Gordy warned people from his crew to stay out of the way." Penny whispered as the filming was going on. "I'm not even going to watch the ending; I lived it and want to forget it. I hope Tia can separate herself from the crime." I knew Penny had a hard time doing that, but her nightmares were starting to get less frequent.

Penny said she was going to her dressing room till it was over, I said I'd come by then. She went off with Willy and I went to Wayne when he called me. We talked about the scene in the prop room where Penny was tied to the bed. They allowed Tia a little more clothing cover than Penny had back then, it was better for her and the scene. I explained to Wayne what happened in detail that day and he was happy. He went to film the scene and they shot it from different angles and then it was finished. It was a little hard for me to see the actor playing me shoot the Davey actor, I still have a chill when I think of killing a person, even if he was a murderer. Wayne yelled that it was in the can and the actors playing the principle roles all were cheering the way it went and then they headed back to the bus that transported them here. The next scenes filmed would be the hospital where Trapper shot Alice Stone. The crew had built the hospital room at the studio since the real hospital wouldn't allow filming there.

I went to Penny's dressing room, she was sitting with a couple of her staff groupies, reading a book and Willy was on her lap sleeping. I greeted the groupies, and then Willy saw me and jumped down to bounce around at my feet. I picked him up and told Penny they had finished all the filming here. It was three hours later and Penny was getting antsy to leave. We went back to where they were finishing packing the equipment, found Tia, Trapper and Earl and we all went to our cars and drove back to the studio.

Wendell was standing guard at the door and greeted us as we trooped in. "They have the hospital all set up, it's amazing the realism that they can do." He smiled. I said welcome to the world of fantasy. Two other security guards came up and Wendell introduced them, Ben Keller and Ted Stoddard. They both were older men like Wendell and I, but Ted looked in better shape of the three. Wendell said that they were to watch Tia carefully in case the killer shows. I said that was good and watched the two guards follow Tia to her dressing room. I took Penny and our boys to the sidelines where they had comfortable cloth folding chairs for our use and we sat.

187

Made for TV Murders

Wayne examined the hospital room and was satisfied with it. He called the actors playing Buck, Trapper and me over to cover the scene and they ran through it a couple times while Wayne watched to see what worked best. He conferred with the cinematographer and they made a couple takes from different angles. Tia was lying in the bed, probably sleeping by now. The actress playing Alice Stone-Morgan was standing by for her part and they made a couple takes of various close-ups and then they did the scene where Buck and I came into the room finding Alice standing over Penny's bed.

The actors were running their lines just as there was a popping sound and the side of the pillow next to Tia's head suddenly exploded. Earl and Trapper knew what had happened and had their guns out running to where the sound originated. I ran to Tia and pulled her from the bed and on to the floor, covering her the best I could with my gun drawn. Everyone in the crew was now scattering, running for cover. I suddenly realized that I had left Penny sitting on her chair and turned to yell for her to get down but she was gone. I looked around the room and saw that Wendell had Penny covered by his body standing by a wall; I'd have to thank Wendell later.

I could hear Earl and Trapper yelling to each other, then I told Tia to get under the bed, she did. I stood and looked around to see if I could see anything from where the shot came from. One of the two security guards who were supposed to be guarding Tia came running up and I said to stay with her. I went over to the side and saw

Trapper up in the catwalk for the overhead lights and Earl was scouting around the riggings and sets. Trapper yelled to Earl that he found a spent shell casing, from a forty caliber handgun on the walkway. He had it in his handkerchief and brought it down. Earl yelled asking if anyone saw who was up in the catwalk. No one answered.

"Damn, this is not good. We really need to tighten up our security." Earl was not happy that someone took a shot at Tia. I went back to the guard watching Tia as she came out from under the bed, and asked where Ted Stoddard was. Ben said he had to use the rest room, since they were busy filming, he went off. I looked around then saw Stoddard coming out of the hallway door from where the rest rooms were. He came over and Ben told him what happened, he looked shocked.

Tia was shaking now as Penny comforted her and they went off to her dressing room followed by the guards. I yelled for them to keep watching around in case the shooter comes back. Wayne was in shock, he asked me if it was wise to continue, I said we'd see. Earl had already called his men and Trapper was blocking the door to the outside and told Wendell to block the front door so no one left.

Earl yelled for everyone in the studio to assemble by the director's office door. There were about eighty people gathered and Earl asked if anyone knew if anyone else was missing. They took a count and everyone was there.

Made for TV Murders

Earl came over to Trapper and me standing by the exit door and said, "Either the killer is one of these people or an outsider sneaking around. That damn phantom of the movie studio again."

Trapper said he didn't see anyone go out the door and there were no other exits other than the big over head doors where the trucks unloaded, and they were closed. The killer had to be in the studio still. Earl said the conference room was big enough for everyone to sit in and yelled to Scott Bailey to gather everyone in that room. The studio was empty now except for Wayne, Penny and the principle actors who sat in Wayne's office. Earl's men had arrived and he filled them in on events, putting two men guarding the crew and two men guarding the actors. He spread the rest around to search the place and see if they could find anyone hiding out. About five minutes later, CSU showed up and Earl wanted them to take a GSR test on everyone in the crew room, if anyone fired a gun the GSR test would show it. They went to the room and proceeded to test everyone.

"Okay, everyone had a job to do while filming, but someone took the time to crawl up to the catwalk and take a shot at Tia. This person doesn't feel right for being one of the crew." Earl surmised. Trapper agreed and said he watched the crew first before searching for the shooter and no on came back from the sides. Everyone he saw was standing around the hospital set.

I said, "The only person who was not in the studio was one of the guards, who was in the rest room, but that meant he would have to cross the studio to get to the rest rooms. We would have seen him."

The CSU men finally came out and said everyone was clean, no gun shot residue on anyone. Earl said to go up to the catwalk where Trapper found the shell and take a look, they went as Trapper showed them were to start, then he came back and joined us.

Earl took me and Trapper aside and said he had an idea on how to draw out the killer. He told us of his plan and it sounded good to us. I went to get Wayne and Scott Bailey and brought them over to tell them of our plan. They reluctantly agreed and said they would have the sets finished being built for the murder scenes by tomorrow morning. After Earl's men came back with no news, Earl told Wayne he could finish the hospital scenes and he would have his men watch from the sides.

The crew was let back in and Wayne announced that they would do this quickly and break for the day so everyone can get their nerves settled. He said he was going to go hit a six pack of beer. I said I'd join him.

The hospital scene was filmed with no more trouble, they were finished with the hospital set, and Wayne announced that tomorrow the extra scenes of the murders of the cheerleaders would be filmed to get it done and over, but with a smaller crew. He said that Scott would post a call sheet for those who would work tomorrow; everyone else was excused for the day. He thanked everyone and said to go get some rest, but said to the set construction crew to get busy striking the hospital set, they had a long night to go to build the crime scene sets.

Trapper sent his men off and they were followed by the CSU men who said they found nothing at all to help.

I went to Wayne and Scott and said they did their parts well. Wayne and Scott said they'd be in early to be sure the sets were built and ready to go. Earl said he'd have his people in and they'd go over the plan, and hope it worked.

*

Chapter 28

Buck was sitting with Celeste and Luther at his dining table, relaxing, talking about the movie.

"Man, now I have to track down all my relatives and tell them I'm in a real movie and I even got lines to speak, damn." Luther exclaimed when Celeste asked how he felt about the filming.

Boon came in the front door and said that everyone had packed up and cleaned up the front yard and were ready to head out. Buck, Celeste and Luther got up from the table and went out with Boon.

"You sure you don't want us around another day in case Tony Marco shows up again?" Luther asked Buck as they went to the choppers.

"Appreciate it Luther, but I think we can handle it from here. You take care and thanks, if I need you I know where you live." Buck grinned and shook Luther's hand. He waved to everyone as they kicked on the cycles and started to head out the drive. Buck and Celeste watched for a bit as the parade rode down the highway, then Buck turned to Celeste, "Feel like staying one more night here, just to be different?" She agreed and said she was going to cook Buck dinner.

~~*~~

It was just now around 6:30 and my posse was tired from the long day so we went to the cars and started to head home. Trapper and Earl agreed to go to their own homes and let us rest. Earl said he was first going to go by his precinct and set his plan in motion, it would take a bit of arranging, but he'd have everything ready for tomorrow morning. Trapper offered to come and help, Earl said that he'd like that, and they walked off chattering about the plan. I took Penny, Willy and Tia to the car, as I looked back to the building I saw Wendell standing at the door watching us. I told the women that I had something to do and went back to Wendell.

"Hey, chief, I want to thank you for protecting Penny earlier, it was good of you. I owe you." I said.

Made for TV Murders

He smiled and said, "It was my pleasure, I'd hate to see either of the ladies get hurt."

"Well, thanks again." I said and shook his hand, he had no strength in his grip, he really needed to work out. I smiled and said we'd see him in the morning. He said he'd be there, at his post. I turned and went to the car, driving my precious cargo back to our home.

~~*~~

Buck went to the bathroom to take a quick shower while Celeste was busy making a dinner out of what she could find in the kitchen. Buck savored in the warm water and finished scrubbing his body, then reaching for the towel just outside of the curtains. He dried off and went through the door that was open to his bedroom and pulled on a pair of jeans and a t-shirt with a big Harley logo on it. He slipped into a pair of loafers and looked at himself in the mirror behind the dresser. He smiled and went out the bedroom door to the hall and out to the kitchen. He came in but Celeste was not there, and a pan with pork chops was burning on the stove. Buck turned off the stove and moved the pan to another burner. He yelled for Celeste but heard nothing. He started to panic and went to the back door and found it open, he ran to the dining table where he had left his .38 and picking it up he went back to the door and burst through it. He stood listening for any noise around the backyard and thought he heard thrashing from the bush in the next property. He ran that way and then heard a muffled scream. His heart was pounding in his chest as he flailed through the tall weeds and brush of

194

the vacant lot that earlier he and the rest of the men had stormed into chasing Tony Marco.

Ahead of Buck was Tony Marco trying to pull and drag an uncooperative Celeste through the nasty brush heading for his car parked back by the road. Marco had driven off earlier trying to avoid the gun fire of the men and then he drove about a mile down the highway and pulled onto a side street and waited patiently for everyone to leave. When he saw the motorcycles and cars drive by he waited then came back to Buck's property. Parking back in the same place, he came to the back of the house and found Celeste in the kitchen. He grabbed her and pulled her out the door and to the property edge. Celeste wasn't making it easy for him and he couldn't use his gun since he fired off all his ammo earlier, so it was just extra weight for him to carry. Buck was tearing through the brush, then started bellowing at the top of his lungs for Marco to stop. Tony heard Buck now and turned with Celeste in front of him as Buck came flying out of the brush with his weapon pointing towards the two people.

"Go ahead and shoot, kill the bitch you fucking freak." Tony yelled as he managed to pull out a large folding knife and flipped it open with one hand as he had done many times before. He brought it up to Celeste's neck and said, "Now what you big freak? Want to play with her life?" He kept Celeste between him and Buck, slowly moving backwards towards the car now just feet away.

Made for TV Murders

Tony brought the knife up higher on Celeste's neck and she cried out in pain. "Drop the gun, freak or I'll slit her throat wide open!" He yelled.

"What the fuck for? Why are you even doing this? Is she really worth you dying for, because if you slit her throat, I'll blow your fucking head off, then I'll shoot your balls just for the fun of it." Buck screamed.

Tony pulled the knife tighter and Buck could see blood starting to trickle down from her throat. Buck had to make a decision, he brought the gun down but still held it. Marco yelled to throw it off to the side, Buck did. Buck had been walking slowly towards the two of them as he was talking and now he was about ten feet away. Celeste looked to Buck and he winked at her, nodding his head. Celeste brought her right foot up high and brought it down hard on Tony's foot, causing him to scream in pain and loosen up on Celeste just enough for her to break loose.

Buck took the opening and crashed into Tony pushing him back against the car. Buck hadn't seen Tony other than a brief glimpse earlier, so he was a bit surprised by Tony's size and power he had. The two men were both full of muscles and it would be a close fight. Buck lifted Tony up and dropped him with a body slam on the ground, glancing off the fender of the car. Tony was stunned as Buck wrestled him to his stomach to get a hold on him. Buck had forgotten that Tony still had the knife and Tony found an opening to bring the knife up and into Buck's shoulder. Buck yelled from the pain he felt from the cut and swung at Tony hitting him in the

196

head as hard as he could. Tony turned over managing to get his feet up and into Buck's groin and pushed him off. Buck flew back and came down hard on the ground. Tony scrambled up and held on to the knife in a stabbing grasp running to Buck and was about to plunge the knife into Buck when there came an small explosion and Tony flew backwards looking stunned. Buck tilted his head up and saw Celeste had picked up his gun and blasted Tony. She fired it again as he tried to lunge forward again with the knife. The second blast took him down and Buck jumped up to get the gun from Celeste before she ripped into him any more. Tony laid still; Buck went to him and checked, he was dead.

Buck pulled out his cell phone and speed dialed Handley and told him what had happened, Handley said to call the locals and he'd try to get there as quickly as possible. Handley hung up and Buck went to Celeste who was sitting on the ground now. He sat next to her and put his arm around her, she put her head on his shoulder and stared at the body before her, not believing what she had done.

The New Baltimore cops had arrived from Buck's call and Handley came flying up in a patrol car driven by a uniformed officer, with flashers and sirens. Handley and the local officer on the scene chatted a bit then the coroner had taken the body away after forensics did their thing. EMS had bandaged up Buck's shoulder and Celeste's neck, just a minor cut they said, but an inch over it could have been serious. After the locals had left, Buck, Celeste, Handley and the uniform sat on the picnic table in Buck's front yard.

"Well, it was a good shoot, self-defense and saved your butt, big guy." Handley smiled.

'Yeah, well I would have taken care of him, but it worked out for the better." Buck gave Celeste his walrus smile.

Handley looked to Celeste and said, "That foot stomp was a great move, good you thought of it."

"Actually I have Buck to thank for that." she said and continued as Handley looked confused, "Back at my apartment I asked Buck what should I do if ever attacked and he showed me a few moves. The foot stomp was one of them. I was scared but when Buck winked and nodded at me I remembered his training." She smiled.

Buck said, "I should go into teaching self-defense training for women," and gave his trademark smile.

*

Chapter 29

We were plopped out on the couch with chips, beer and TV. I was enjoying my relaxation when my cell phone rang. It was on the snack bar counter so I had to get up and went to see that Buck was calling.

"Hey boss, what's up?" I asked.

"Well, our stalker is dead." Was all he said, I waited for the other shoe to be thrown.

"Ok, why'd you kill him?" I asked.

He laughed and said, "Nope, wasn't me, Celeste blasted him with my gun. It was a righteous shoot too."

He proceeded to explain the events of the evening and I just listened. He got into the graphic nature of the crime and how Celeste saved the day and possibly his life. I said I was proud of her and he could go home now. He reminded me that he was at home and would have to take Celeste back to her home. He asked me how my murders were doing, I told him about the attempt on Tia today and he asked if I wanted him to come in to help watch for the killer. I said it wouldn't be a bad idea if he wanted to come down and watch the festivities tomorrow, may even help to catch our killer. Buck said he'd be there and he'd bring Celeste with him for the hell of it. I said he'd have to watch her; we were going to try and draw out the killer. He said he'd watch her; I laughed and said it sounds like she should watch over him. He snorted and hung up.

I went back to the couch and told the women about Buck's adventures and they listened intently. It was getting late and we had a long day tomorrow, possibly catching our killer, so we all exchanged good-nights and went off to bed. Penny and I did a quick sailor and the hooker fantasy and then crawled under the covers to sleep. I didn't sleep very well, thinking about the events of the day and Buck's adventures. I finally drifted off and dreamt about having to act in the movie but I didn't know my lines.

Morning came early and with a storm. Penny had to go to her station and I said it would be good if she didn't come to the studio today, as she was threatened by the killer too. She went off with Willy, while Tia and I got our stuff together and drove to the studio. We arrived and I dropped her at the door to keep from getting soaked in the rain. I pulled out the umbrella I kept under the seat and made a beeline to the side door. Wendell was standing just inside the entrance and he greeted me, saying that Earl had requested me to come to the conference room. I went down the hall and into the room and found about ten people sitting or standing around the room. There were three women being fitted with Kevlar vests and then they put on the costumes that the actresses would have worn. I was getting the idea, but Trapper explained they were female cops who would be playing the parts of the actresses playing the murder victims. The rest of the men were real cops, going to play the bit players in the film. Earl had told Wayne to tell everyone that the actors were being protected and kept in the conference room till needed and not to tell anyone they were cops.

Earl had called in Wayne and Scott and asked if the crew was ready. They said they had the people on Earl's list of possible suspects assigned to work crew today.

The rest were excused, but if the killer was one of them, they would still have to get into the building.

Wayne, Scott, Earl, Trapper and I went out to the studio and Scott called the crew over and Wayne announced that all the actresses who were supposed to be in the film had quit but they found replacements. Earl had about four uniformed police in to act the part of watching the crew but he told them to do a lousy job so the killer wouldn't be frightened off. They didn't take that well, but agreed to act normal.

Wayne and I walked around the new sets, built during the night. The salon where Sue Carter had her throat slit, the bed room where Linda Gorlich got stabbed and the kennel set that was still waiting to be filmed. Wayne announced that they would do the Salon shoot first since it was the most complex of the three. He called for the actors and the Buck actor and my clone came out of the conference room. The female cop who was going to play Sue Carter had experience in acting and was given her lines last night, so she had time to get ready. The shoot went well, as we watched around the set. I told Earl that since Sue Carter had her throat slit, our killer would have to get near her to do the job. All the cops pretending to be actors did their part well, and the actress who was playing Alice Stone-Morgan did her part as the old woman. Wayne said they'd shoot the outdoor scenes tomorrow.

The interior scenes of the salon were all filmed and finished and Wayne was happy despite the fact that his actors were police. I noted that all the cops were really getting into their roles.

I heard a commotion at the entrance and looked over to see Wendell holding Buck back from coming in. I went over and introduced Buck and Celeste to Wendell and he apologized to Buck. I took the two of them over and let them sit on the folding chairs and gave Buck a briefing on what was going on. I smiled at Tia who was sitting on a folding chair next to Celeste; she was flanked by the two security guards that I met yesterday. They gave me a grim smile; at least they tried to smile.

Wayne called me over to ask me about the bedroom scene, but I said I wasn't there so he'd have to confer with Trapper on that. He did. Wayne quietly asked the female cop who played Sue to go and get the female cop to play Linda Gorlich. I watched her go to the hallway door and down to the conference room. I could see from my vantage the full hallway, and shortly the woman playing Linda came out of the room. As she came down the hall I saw her look to the woman's restroom and then went in. I grabbed Trapper and told him to follow. We went through the door into the hall and to the restroom. I opened the door and yelled in for the woman and she answered.

"Are you all right?" I asked.

She said, "I'm fine just a little nervous about being in this movie."

"Are you alone in there?" I asked. She said she was and I waited with Trapper till she came out. She apologized for the diversion and we went out to the studio.

She really didn't look like she was in her sixties, but make-up did their best to age her. She went to the set and they did a run through for everyone and had the Davey actor, in costume with ski mask, get into the closet, ready for his kill. Wayne called for a take and they filmed the scene up to the knifing of her in the heart. They did a couple of close-ups of the hands over her chest and the plunge. The knife hit the Kevlar and stopped, Davey look surprised. The knife blade was supposed to retract into the handle but it didn't and Wayne jumped forward along with Earl to check the knife. It wasn't the one that was supposed to be used, it was real. Earl took the knife in his handkerchief and called for Jane, the prop person again and asked her about it. She was confused because she had checked it before the take and it collapsed properly.

Earl looked to "Davey" and said, "Have you had this knife since Jane gave it to you?"

He looked at the knife and said, "I did set it down briefly to put on this mask, it was the only time I didn't have it".

"Where did you set it?"

"I put it on that table over there," pointing to a table near where Wendell was sitting at his post, "while I stood by the table talking to that guard."

Earl and Trapper went to Wendell and asked if he watched the actor put the knife on the table. Wendell looked surprised and said he had placed it there, but it was in full view at all times or so he thought. Earl called one of the uniform cops over and said to take Wendell to one of the offices and keep him there till he could talk to him. Wendell was upset but went with the cop as they went to an office next to Wayne's.

I asked Earl if he thought Wendell could have done something to it. Earl said, "Either he or the Davey actor where the only ones around it, but then Jane said she gave the collapsing knife to Davey, but could she be lying? Okay, we have to sort this out. But I think we need to eliminate them by going on with the filming and seeing if anything more happens."

He told Wayne to go ahead and finish the scene and Jane came up with another trick knife just before Earl asked her to go to the room with Wendell and the cop. She made a face but went.

"Okay we've eliminated two suspects, we watch Davey real close now."

Wayne called for a take of the rest of the scene and they finished it without problems.

*

Chapter 30

Earl had called in CSU and asked them to bring their new fingerprint toy with them. I had heard him ask that and when he finished the call I asked him what it was. He said they had purchased these new devices that can scan a finger and radio the print back to the computers at the precinct and run it for ID. He said the patrol cars would get them to use for on the scene ID of people. I was impressed.

Wayne called for a break and Earl asked everyone to stay close, no one was to leave the building. The small crew just sat in an area set up for breaks where they all could be watched. About fifteen minutes later, CSU came in and Earl took them to the room with his prime suspects. He gave them the knife and asked if they could do a quick run on any prints that turn up on the knife and also compare it to the people in the room and send it in for a check. They said they'd do their best, and we went back out to the studio and waited.

About twenty minutes later, the lead CSU officer came out and went to Earl, sitting on a folding chair next to Tia. He said something into Earl's ear and Earl stood motioning to Trapper and me to follow. We went into the office and I saw Wendell sitting looking upset. The lead CSU said they managed to get a good partial off the blade by the hilt and ran it through the scanner. It came back with a hit, from the Chesterfield Police fingerprint database of people who registered weapons and had to give their prints. Earl looked at the printout and looked to me with a slightly surprised expression.

"This thing says the print belongs to Robert Morgan. Sound familiar?"

I was stunned, "But I thought Bob Morgan killed himself by carbon monoxide?"

"That's what the coroner's report said, but evidently they had the wrong body. Something is hinkey here."

"Okay, if Morgan is alive that explains a lot. But, I've met and talked to Morgan and I didn't see him here unless he's disguised. If one of the people here is Morgan, let's take that scanner out and shake him up." I said. Earl caught my idea and we took the CSU people out with us. Wendell was cleared to go along with Davey.

Earl yelled for everyone to assemble and explained that we had a killer but needed to narrow down who he is. He explained about the device and that everyone was to be printed to compare to the killer's print. He told everyone to line up and I was standing back watching for anyone bolting for an exit. The plan had worked, for one of the security guards, Ted Stoddard, who was watching Tia suddenly was walking towards the back of a set. I yelled to Trapper and Earl and pointed the way. Earl yelled to his uniforms to watch everyone as we went in pursuit of the fleeing guard.

We ran around the set and saw Stoddard running towards the back of the studio, but it was a dead end. I don't think he realized that as he looked confused and turned to run in a different direction, but as he came around a set, Wendell was standing in front of him and tackled him low to the legs. They both went down as Trapper and Earl pounced on him and cuffed him. I helped Wendell up and thanked him for his heroics.

We took Stoddard, or Morgan, back to the office and the CSU ran his print and it came up positive. I looked closely at his face and could see the face of Morgan beneath scaring around his head that told me he had surgery to change his appearance.

"Morgan you were gutsy to pull this off, why did you do it?" Trapper asked.

"Fuck you Trapper, you killed my Alice, I wanted to save you for last after I took out Richards." he spit out.

"Why kill the actresses?" I asked.

"They represented the women who led my darling to do what she had to do. I couldn't let them live knowing they were glorifying the crimes the cheerleaders committed, or let this movie be made to make my love look bad. But it's all right; the last of the cheerleaders is getting her due."

I had a chill about that and asked him what he meant, he remained silent. I pulled out my cell phone and called Penny; it rang a number of times and went to voice mail. I looked at my watch and she should have been done with the taping of her show by now. I called Gordy and he came on and I asked if Penny was still there. He said that one of the staff brought a note to her about an hour ago and she went out of the studio. He didn't know where she went. I asked if he could put security on her trail, I think she may have been kidnapped. He sounded stunned and said he'd have everyone looking and call me back.

I went to Morgan and grabbed his lapels and pulled him up and pushed him against the wall. "If I find out Penny is in danger, you will regret it, I swear I will tear you apart with my bare hands, you hear me fucker? Talk, where is Penny!?"

He just gave me a deathly stare and didn't say a word. I struck him in the gut and he doubled over. Earl and Trapper pulled me back from him as I tried to stomp him some more.

Earl said, "We should go to the studio and see if we can trail Penny."

I screamed, "to where? We can't run all over the county looking for her, they'd have to have a place to meet to finish her off. I think it's Alice Morgan the second who is behind this." I was watching Morgan and I saw a flinch in his eyes that gave me the hope. "Okay where would they meet, I think back at Alice's home in Chesterfield." I saw another flinch in his eyes. "Yes, he just told me what I wanted to know." I started out the door, Earl grabbed my arm and said we'd take a patrol car and called for his uniforms to meet out in the parking lot. I told Buck to watch Tia and Celeste as we went out of the building, he said he would.

We drove up Gratiot Avenue all the way from Eight Mile Road, with flashers and sirens blaring. We passed through four cities before we hit the Chesterfield border. I directed Earl as to where to go and we arrived at the house where Alice lived. All the patrol cars pulled up and everyone got out. Earl said we couldn't just go busting in without a warrant or probable cause. Just as he said that there was gun fire from the house just missing us. We all took cover behind the cars and I yelled to Earl, "Is that probable cause."

We looked cautiously around the cars and saw the front window to what I presumed was a bedroom, was open and I could almost see a woman inside. We heard a female voice from inside yelling for us to leave or she'd kill Penny. My heart skipped a beat and I looked to Earl. I felt helpless, but I crouched low and went around the next cop car and went off to the side by some bushes, where she couldn't see from her window. I looked behind me and Trapper was there, following me. We went to the back of the house and I looked for a way in but it would be risky and I didn't know what condition Penny was in.

We went up to the building and I carefully looked in the back door window and I could see through the kitchen to the living room. I saw Penny tied up and lying on the floor, so I knew Alice was not near her. I tried the door and it was locked. Trapper told me to move and he brought out a small wallet and took out lock picks. He started working on the door as we heard more gun fire from the front of the house. It would distract from what we were doing. I crouched and watched Trapper at the lock and kept an eye out for Alice in case she may have heard us. I had my Glock in hand and was hoping she would pop up.

Trapper managed to work the lock and he slowly opened the door and proceeded to enter the kitchen. I followed close behind and I could see Penny was facing us and saw us now. She had tape over her mouth and was in her side. I went to her carefully out in the living room as Trapper was crouched low watching down the hall towards the bedrooms where we presumed Alice to be. I put my Glock back in its holster and took out my pocket knife to cut Penny loose. Just as I did that Penny looked shocked as she stared behind Trapper. I saw her expression and looked to Trapper and saw Alice standing in the kitchen, having come around through the back bedroom. She was aiming her gun at Trapper and I did the fastest draw of my Glock that I ever done and blasted over Trappers head hitting Alice full in the chest. Trapper spun and brought his gun up and fired as she was still pointing the gun, shooting it at the ceiling as she went down.

I looked at Trapper who turned back to me as I said, "Well, there goes the last chance for the Morgans."

*

Chapter 31

The Chesterfield Police had made their presence known, someone in the neighborhood called them when the gun play started. Earl and Trapper were explaining the circumstances and they had a coroner in to take the body. I felt bad for Alice, but she made her choices. Penny was just about a wreck and I had her sitting in the patrol car that brought us, I was sitting next to her as she was trying to rest. I called Buck after a while and told him to tell Tia that Penny was safe and Alice Morgan was history.

Earl and Trapper came over and said that they'd take us back to the movie studio and to our car. Penny's car was still at her station, but I said I would take her to work tomorrow and she could drive it home, if she felt better. She asked for my phone and called her station to talk to her make-up girls and asked if they had Willy since she ran out without him, they said he was safe. She explained to me that she got a note saying that I was shot and there was a car waiting to take her to where I was supposed to be, she panicked and rushed out not thinking. I said Willy would be safe with her girls.

We got back to the studio and everyone greeted us. They had already taken Bob Morgan in to be booked and locked away, hopefully for good. Wendell came up and I put my arm around his shoulder and said he did good and I would make a stink to his bosses that he deserved a raise and a promotion. He smiled at me and said that would be real nice. Buck came over and said they had filmed a bit more and Wayne told me they were about done except for a few outdoor scenes.

I said I had enough movie making and I wanted to take my girls home and crack open a good number of beers and just chill. Wayne said he was done with Tia for now and told everyone to quit for the night, tomorrow they could finish a few more scenes without fear now.

I drove Penny and Tia back to the house and we went in. Penny said she wanted to go stand in the shower for about an hour and I said I'd check on her if she wasn't out by then. She smiled and kissed me, asking if I could quit this business, she smiled again and headed off to the bathroom.

Tia went to the kitchen and said she was going to make us something for dinner, I didn't stop her. It was that or order pizza, but Tia had her heart set on making dinner for us. About forty minutes later Penny came out in a robe and sat on the couch next to me as I was watching her show today on the TiVo. It was about relieving stress from our lives and I looked to her as she broke out laughing. We enjoyed the sumptuous meal Tia proudly prepared and then about an hour later, Penny's groupies had brought our baby back, Willy was a bit put off but he survived.

Bob Moats

The film was finished now except for post production, editing and such. Wayne and his staff came to our home as Penny and I invited everyone else to have a picnic out back, and we invited the entire crew who all came in the company bus. We celebrated the end of the hard work everyone put in and had a good time eating and drinking and talking about the crimes. Buck had brought Celeste and they sat with Luther and his crew who came also. The crowd was a bit much, but it was fun.

I asked Becker to bring his magic equipment and give us a show. I got everyone's attention and explained what was going to happen and I turned it over to Barry who did a fine job with his act. He decided to get into comedy magic which made me happy as it was what I used to do. Since we got back from the magic convention, I gave him a number of pointers on how to have fun with the audience but not insult them. He did well for his first time out. Trapper told me as we sat watching that he was fond of Becker, I had already known that, just by the way he always watched over Barry. Becker finished and everyone gave him a standing ovation. He grinned from ear to ear.

About two months later and after I took a vacation from crime fighting, the movie was finished. They were going to have a premiere of the film at the Fox Theatre in Detroit before the film went to television. I hoped everyone would survive the almost three and a half hour film. We all dressed up and Tia flew back in from California with her secret husband. Trapper and Earl were a bit put off by the man in her life, but they got over it. Buck brought Celeste; they were getting along pretty well, and were visiting each other more often. I wondered if there might be a romance, but Buck said his heart still belonged to Maria out in Vegas. Deacon and Lynn flew in from Vegas for the showing and we even had a red carpet rolled out front for all the actors and crew. There were all the local television news crews on hand to document the affair. When everyone was in and seated, we all sat back enjoying the film. They had put in the end credits a dedication to the actors who lost their lives while filming this movie and a dedication to all the real people who had lived it and lost their lives also. Howard had rented a local hall and had an after premiere party and it went well into the night.

The next day everyone went back to their lives, Deacon and Lynn had to get back; crime in Vegas didn't stop for a movie. It was good to see them again. The film crew had all headed back to California and the actors went on to other parts. We had fond memories, well not of the murders, but the good times.

Bob Morgan went to trial and was easily convicted of murder and accessory to kidnapping, he was going to be put away for a very long time. He finally confessed that he harbored a hatred for over a year about the killing of his wife, the original Alice Stone and had managed to carefully warp the mind of his niece to help avenge her death at the hands of the cheerleaders and the police who he held equally responsible. He and his niece had manage to find a homeless man in Detroit who matched Morgan's physical build and height along with looks, took him in pretending to want to help the man and then had gotten him drunk then placed him in the car and left him to die of carbon monoxide. Morgan hid out afterwards in Alice's home, and she identified the dead man as her uncle. No one questioned it since young Alice was the only relative, so the authorities accepted the homeless man as Bob Morgan. Morgan became totally withdrawn now knowing he had led his niece to her death and he was to blame. He would suffer for the life sentence he received.

I told Penny it was all so tragic that Sue Carter had started this all in motion when she could have just left it alone all those years ago. Penny and I sat quietly on the couch, Willy lying on my lap sleeping. I looked to Penny and said I was still working on the Vegas showgirl murder book, maybe they could make a film of that too. She looked at me and said if I finish that book she would divorce me. I smiled and kissed her nose.

The End.

For every ending there's a new beginning.

Made for TV Murders

Watch for Jim and Penny returning in "Mystery Cruise Murders" about death at a mystery writer's convention aboard a cruise liner on the Pacific Ocean.

Preview from "Mystery Cruise Murders"

Chapter 1

The woman sat on the hard bench looking up at the can of energy drink, beckoning her to take it. She reached up and not caring that it wasn't hers, popped the pull tab and took a hearty swallow of the liquid, ready to savor the taste. After she had swallowed, her taste buds started to burn, then her stomach started to turn on her, she felt a nauseous dizziness and a foam rose from her throat to her lips. She looked to her friend standing close and tried to talk but couldn't because she was now convulsing. She knew she was dying.

I sat back in my aging desk chair studying the last line I had typed into my laptop remembering how Penny threatened me with divorce if I finished this book about the Vegas showgirl murders, but it had to be told. Okay, it didn't have to be told, but I was really enjoying writing. Penny was kidding me about the fact that my first book brought out murders at the movie studio where the thing was being filmed. She wanted to be sure that no more murders occurred because of my books. My first book, Classmate Murders, had done well in sales, enough to be on the best seller book list and the TV movie made from the book had helped those sales.

Two weeks ago all our friends and family had sat in our living room as we watched the first episode of the two-part miniseries, it was still good even though we had already seen it at the premiere showing at the Fox Theatre in Detroit last Month. We gathered again the next night and finished the show. It did well in the ratings for a cable show, and probably would be going to DVD in a month or so, if it didn't warrant a rerun. I had heard some rumors about it being picked up by one of the networks for prime time viewing. More book sales I thought.

I looked out my office window, it was snowing now, I hated winters. I have absolutely no use for snow or cold and this made me want to move back to Vegas all the more. When the snow first started early this year, Penny and I talked more about moving, it was still on the table, but we just couldn't take that first step to do so. Don't know why, maybe it's because our friends were here and my family, so we had to consider that. Being two thousand miles away from everyone was something to think about and not everyone would move with us.

I turned back to the laptop and thought about my next line in the story, being amazed that people do this without a real life crime to fall back on. I didn't have to make this up, it actually happened, I just had to do it justice with my words. My book was a true crime story with a touch of fictional account, but there were authors out there that had to totally depend on their imagination to create a story that they could put down on paper. I could write, but could I make it up. I'd have to try a fictional book next. I spent the next half hour working on the book until my office door opened, startling me from my concentration. It was Buck.

"Hey Jimmy, what's happening?" He said with a big smile that always brightened my day.

"Just working on my next book." I replied.

"I thought Penny was going to dump you if you finished that book?"

"I'm not telling her."

"She'll know; you know she'll know."

"You're not helping. Did you stop in to tell me something or just to annoy?"

"I just came by to tell you that I talked to Maria last night and she's coming out to stay with me for a month."

"She's leaving Las Vegas to come to this miserable weather?"

"She used to live here, so she wants to play in the snow for a while and spend some time with me." He grinned again. "She said she hasn't been around snow in years and got some vacation time from the Tropicana, so she'll be here in two days."

218

"Is Deacon coming too?"

"No, he's not. Maria warned him not to follow her. He's just a bit overly protective of his sister." Buck laughed.

"And he lets her be with you? I'm astonished."

"So, have you gotten any money from your book sales?" Buck asked ignoring my comment.

"They send me a check every so often, I'm not getting rich, the publishers, bookstores and distributors take their cuts. Amazing how everyone dips into the thing. My book is selling for $29.95 in most good bookstores; I get $3.98 from each book sold, amazing."

"Well, when your book is selling in the millions, you'll be rich." Buck smiled.

"So have you figured what to do with Maria when she comes out, any plans yet?"

"I got all kinds of ideas and places to go. I sat and wrote down nice things to do."

"This isn't Vegas; there isn't a hell of a lot of things to do. Take her to see the closed down factories and stores, or drive up and down the freeway and watch the road rage." I laughed.

Made for TV Murders

"Hey, there are things to do, museums, Henry Ford's Greenfield Village, Detroit Institute of Art, lots of good stuff and we can head north to Frankenmuth and take in the German restaurants along with Bronner's Christmas store."

"I know there are things to do and I'm sure you'll be able to entertain her for the month. If you two can get out of the bedroom."

"It's not about sex, which is good, but not the only thing... well, its most of it." He gave a sly little smile.

Just as he finished saying that my office door opened and a woman stepped in. She looked at Buck and me and had a confused expression. I stood.

"May I help you?" I asked as I came around the desk towards her.

"I'm looking for Jim Richards." she said quietly like she didn't want to disturb us.

"I'm he. Can I help you?" I said again.

"May we talk?" she asked looking at Buck.

"Come in, this is Buck Carson, my associate in crime fighting." I said.

Her face brightened and she went to Buck. "Mr. Buck, yes I know of you. I read Mr. Richards's book, Classmate Murders, and I know you." She held her hand out to shake Buck's; he stood and took her hand and did one of those European greetings of kissing her hand. He looked to her and said it was a pleasure to meet such a lovely lady. I didn't think Buck would ever do something like that, but he always surprised me. She flushed and giggled and said, "It's an honor to meet you."

Buck offered her the client chair he was sitting in, she thanked him and sat. He pulled up one of the extra chairs from by the door and sat at the end of my desk. I was still standing, I figured I better sit.

"Now, what can I do for you and your name is?" I asked.

"I'm Elizabeth Collins and I need your help, I'm on the main committee for our writers organization and we have a problem," she started, "I'm with the International Mystery and Horror Writers Association and we have a convention coming up this month and one of our guest speakers has taken ill and can't make it. I've watched your television miniseries and have read your book, we were wondering if you'd be interested in being a speaker? We had our plans all arranged last year and didn't know about you till this last month, and now everyone really wants you to fill in. I know its short notice, but things have happened so fast."

I was a bit taken by surprise that she wanted me, I never thought about becoming a speaker. "What would this entail and where is the convention to be held."

Made for TV Murders

"Well, you'd just have to talk about the classmate crime and how you came to write the book, plus we'd like to hear about your adventures in fighting crimes that have been so widely publicized since the movie. You are quite well known now in our circles. I'm sure our group would gain valuable knowledge from your work. As to where, it's being held on the Queen of the Pacific Ocean liner, sailing from Los Angeles to Hawaii and Tahiti then back. It's a ten day cruise, just for the convention people."

I could see Buck's jaw drop even though he hadn't opened his mouth, my mouth did drop a bit. An ocean cruise, I had never been on one before and the closest I got to one was when I took first place in the magic competition during the magic convention in Colon. I was offered a three month contract to perform my act on a cruise line but turned it down, too long for Penny to be away from her show. Ten days could be arranged if her station ran reruns, they've done it before.

"You would be paid for your time and all air travel expenses to the ship and back to here would be covered. Your cruise, stateroom and food would be covered also. I'm sure you will bring your lovely wife, Penny." She added.

"She'd murder me if I didn't. Well it sounds like an offer I really can't refuse. One condition, may I bring two friends with us, I'd pay for their air travel myself." I said thinking of Buck and Maria. I could see Buck's eyes widen.

"I'm sure it can be arranged, who might your friends be, may I ask?"

"Well, Buck and his lady friend." I told her.

Her eyes shifted to Buck and a smile crept across her mouth. "It would be an honor to have Mr. Buck along." I noticed the mention of a lady friend didn't faze her, I thought Buck may have a stalker now.

We finalized the details and she left. Buck was bouncing in his seat. "I got to call Maria, thanks for inviting us, this will be fantastic."

I laughed and said to hold on, as I picked up my cell phone and made a call. Three rings later Penny answered, I said, "Hi beautiful, pack your bikini, you'll never believe where we are going."

*

Continued in book....

~~*~~

Jim Richards Family of Readers

Thanks to the following people who are now part of the Jim Richards Family of Readers. They have read a book or more and enjoyed them. They all volunteered to be included in the list. If you are a fan of the books, send me your full name and you will be included in future books. Send your name to murdernovels@bobmoats.com to be added here and on the website.

* Achim Feifel * Al Norris * Alex Wheatley * Alexandra Delporte-Wilkinson * Amy Tapia * Andrea Bryan * Anne Shepherd * Arianda Sugar * Arlene Markowski * Ashley Augustus * Audra Hall * Barbara Hughes * Barbara Sammons * Barbara Schuler * Barbara Zirger * Beth Donohue Plenskofski * Betsy Childress * Beth Gibson * Bill Sandy * Bill Tornquist * Billie-jo Collie * Boni J Rychener * Carl Bishopric * Carla Lewis * Carole Henderson * Carolyn Conroy * Carolyn Riddle-Linington * Cassy Bailey * Cathie Turner * Chad Hudson * Charlotte L Duran * Cheryl L. Everett * Cindy Ackley Nunn * Cindy Valstad * Connie Bancroft * Corinne Kay O'Daniel * Dana Robbins Chuchran * Dana Wichita * Danielle Monique * Darren Heald * Dave Travers * David Wilkinson * DeAnn Jannereth * Deanna Miller * Deb Breuker Balbo * Debbie Carter * Debbie White * Deborah Fartuch * Deborah Gauze * Deborah Sullivan * Dee King * Denise Freeman * Diana Carver * Dixie Beck * Donna Gould * Donna Thompson * Donny Minter * Doris Kight

Bob Moats

* Eddie Moore * Eric Walters * Felicia Annette Bradfield
* Francine Menor * Gail Chesney * Georgiann Minster *
George Conner * Greg Colucci * Hayley Rankin * Harold
Garcia * Heidi Arnold * Irma Ranee Coy * Jacqueline
Moss * Jan Kimball * Janice Schneider * Janice Spoor *
Jennifer Redmond * Jessica Keown-Belous * Jim Beck *
Jo Boguslaw * Jo Turner * Joanne Marie Turner * John
Peiffer * John Wisbiski * Joseph Wauro * Joyce Stacy *
Joyce Trifiletti * Judy Franklin * Judy Travers * Judy
Padgett * Julie Heath * Junnahvee Benson * Karen Dahl *
Karen Grams * Karen Higham * Karen Kaiser * Karen
Meinburg Richwine * Karen Kirkman Parker * Karin
Hawkins * Karin Vasvari * Kathleen Donohue Roesing *
Kathleen Riddle-Wolfe * Kathy Hinds Moore * Kathy
Jones * Kathy Mitchell * Katie Benzler * Kay Burns *
Kelly Garcia * Ken Boggs * Keota Rodriguez * Kiera
Mccarthy * Kim Estes * Kitty Stolle * Kristie Sciler *
Kirsty Stanton * LaLonnie Scallen * Larry Morris *
Leann Parr * Lenora Scales * Leslie Marie Jackson *
Linda Forester * Linda Ingle Cox * Linda Kennerö *
Linda Magill * Lisa Bower * Liz Gibson * Lorraine
Wiman * Loretta Alexander * Lynda Bowles * Lynette
Lawrance * LuAnn Louttit * Manny Rothman * Marcia
Gibson DeWitt * Marie Calder * Marlene Bryan *
MaryLouise Kramp * Mary Lynn Gross * Megan Atkins *
Meghan Hyden * Melody Cannavan * Michael Carruthers
* Michael Dinkens * Michael Vannoy * Michelle Burns-
Mitchell * Michelle Pilcher * Micki Potter * Mike Moats
* Mimi Baur * Myrna Hecht * Nadine Sutton * Nancy
Ellen Sayre * Natalie Quine * Neena Martin * O'Della
Wilson * Pat Pollington * Pat Rohn * Patricia Jarmon *
Patricia C Trezza * Patrick Barry * Paul Lawrance *
Peggy Davis * Phyllis Bassett * Raylene Matheny *
Rebecca Collins Besner * Renee Brumley * Reta Hanna *
Reta Moats * Roberta Navarro-Harder * Sally Berneathy *

Made for TV Murders

Sally Hubler * Sarah Santos * Satka Nikc * Sharon E. Edwards * Sharon Mangini * Sharon McMillon * Sheena Rawl * Sherry Amstutz * Shirley Alvarez * Shirley Davies * Shirley Williams * Stacie Rowe * Stephanie Conner * Steve Cullen * Susan Haughton * Susan Hesse Adams * Susan Salomon * Suzan K Chase * Taisha Cullum * Tamara Moore * Tammy Castleberry * Tammy Lynn Wood * Ted Murphy * Terri Atkins * Terri Creech * Terry Raab * Tonia Rachael Riggs-Williams * Travis Fleury-Lopez * Twyla Gawlas * Val Brooks * Walt Munsel * Yvonne Isakson *

Thank you to all these wonderful people.

Thank you for purchasing this book. I hope you enjoy it as much as I enjoyed writing it for my faithful readers. Please feel free to email me to tell me what you thought about my stories. I love hearing from the readers. I can be reached at murdernovels@bobmoats.com thanks again!

*